Beyond The Pecos

By

Norm Bass

First Edition
Published by Hooked B Publishing, January 2013

Copyrighted Material

All rights reserved. No part of this book may be reproduced in any form or by any means without written permission of the author or his representatives.

Preface

Both real and fictional places are named in this book. However, the characters and events portrayed in this book are purely fictional. The story is in no way intended to reflect on any real people including the current or past residents or citizens of any actual places. Any similarities to real events or actual persons are strictly coincidental and should not in any way be considered factual.

Table of Contents

CHAPTER ONE 1

CHAPTER TWO 14

CHAPTER THREE 28

CHAPTER FOUR 47

CHAPTER FIVE 61

CHAPTER SIX 76

CHAPTER SEVEN 88

CHAPTER EIGHT 94

CHAPTER NINE 106

Chapter One

    It was springtime along the Pecos River in the year of 1889. Miguel Ortez was busy making repairs to the goat pen and replacing a few of the rotted wooden posts with new cedar posts that he had cut and hauled all the way from Red Bluff. His wife, Maria, was on the sunny side of their simple two roomed adobe hut, planting the garden that she hoped would provide them with fresh vegetables throughout the year and enough extra to sell in order to subsidize the meager income they earned selling goat cheese and goat meat. Their three month old son, swaddled in a thin blanket, was not far away sleeping soundly in a plain wicker basket on the shady side of the adobe.

    Miguel had just finished digging out the stubborn remains of a rotted post. He leaned the clam shell posthole digger against the shed and removed his sombrero. As he started mopping the sweat from his forehead with a sun bleached bandana, he noticed four men leading a string of horses riding north on the road that paralleled the river. He continued to watch the men as they crossed the river and turned toward his adobe. Miguel's grey stallion whinnied and snorted at the horses as he trotted along the fence line with Miguel's other horse, a sorrel mare, following close behind. As the men got closer to the adobe, Miguel stuffed his bandanna in his back pocket, put on his sombrero, and walked toward the front of the adobe to greet the men. Maria stood up when she heard the pounding hooves of the approaching horses and quickly un-tucked the back of her skirt which she had pulled up between her legs and tucked into her waist band to prevent it from dragging in the dirt. Then she untied the bandana holding back her long, black hair and ran it over her face hoping to erase any dirt smudges that might exist.

    "Good afternoon, amigos," Miguel said with a friendly smile as he looked over the rough looking men and wished that he had thought to bring his shotgun with him.

"Howdy," one of the men replied, as he removed his hat revealing the large scar that started at his hairline and ended behind the black patch that covered his left eye.

Miguel continued looking the men over, but said nothing further as the man with the patch pulled the bandana from around his neck and dried the sweatband inside his well-worn and tattered hat.

"Noticed that gray stallion you got out there. Would you be interested in selling it?"

"No Señor, he is not for sale. Those are my only horses."

"As you can see, I'm in the business of buying and selling horses," the man said smiling.

"I am sorry Señor, but he is not for sale."

"I'll make you a fair offer," the man persisted. "What do you need with two horses anyway?"

"One is for me and the other is for my wife, Señor." Miguel said glancing in the direction of his wife.

"Oh, I see. After noon, Ma'am," the man said loudly with a friendly nod of his head as he noticed Maria in the distance for the first time.

"Well, if you're sure you won't sell him," the man said still smiling as he put on his hat and tied the bandana around his neck. "I reckon…I'll just have to take him!"

The man quickly drew his Colt pistol and shot Miguel in the chest. The bullet spun Miguel around and the man put another bullet in Miguel's back as he fell to the ground. Maria screamed and ran toward her baby, but her loose fitting sandals caught in the loose dirt and she fell to the ground after taking only a few steps. The man spurred his horse into a gallop as the other men cheered and one of them yelled, "Get her Cap!" Maria kicked off her sandals as she scrambled to her feet, but the man was on her before she could take another step. He threw her to the ground and slapped her with the back of his hand. Then laughing, he began tearing off her blouse and then her skirt. Maria raked her nails across the man's face, drawing blood. The man cursed at her and slapped her again, harder, bloodying her nose. Maria continued her desperate attempt to fight her way free, but she was no match for the man who was now sitting on her, pinning her arms to the ground.

"Give me a hand, Sergeant!" the man yelled with an evil laugh. "She's a real wildcat!"

One of the other men dismounted and continued laughing as he walked over to lend a hand with Maria who was out of breath and nearly exhausted, but still struggling to free herself.

"What's the matter, Captain? She too much woman for you?" the man sneered.

"Just hold her down, so I can get my pants down," the man said panting and almost out of breath himself.

The second man pinned Maria down while the man with the patch unbuttoned his pants and then he commenced to rape her as the other three men looked on, laughing, and cheering. Once the man with the patch was finished with Maria, the other men took turns raping her until they each had their fill.

"How about taking her along for later, Cap?" one of the men asked loudly as he lit the cigarette he had just rolled.

"No, we can't risk being seen with her. Besides, we can always get us another Mex," the man with the patch replied as he pulled a large knife from the sheath on his belt and walked over to where Maria lay naked in the freshly turned dirt, curled up in a fetal position, sobbing, but too exhausted to cry. He knelt down beside her and rolled her over. She stared up at him, her eyes filled with terror, her body trembling, dirt caked to her breasts where milk had seeped from her nipples. The man covered her haunting eyes with his left hand and pushed her head back to tighten her neck. She jerked as the razor sharp blade was drawn across her throat and then her body went limp as blood gurgled from her slashed throat. The man chuckled as he wiped the bloodied blade on Maria's bare skin and then he stood up with no hint of emotion on his weathered and unshaven face.

"There must be a damned baby around here someplace," the man said as he joined the other men who were sitting on the porch of the adobe. "That bitch's tits were full of milk."

"I'll check inside," the one who went by the nickname, Sarge, said.

"While you're in there, see if these beaners got anything decent to eat," the man with the patch added loudly. "All that pokin' made me hungry."

On the Double M Ranch, a few miles further downstream, just beyond where the road to Mentone intersected with the road that paralleled the river, Peyote Masters, better known as Punch because of his tendency as a young man to settle things with his fists, was walking back to the ranch house with his son, Luke. They had just finished putting a much needed coat of whitewash on the ornate picket fence that surrounded the five tombstones beneath a large mesquite tree.

Punch's foreman, Duv Smith, and his wife, Angelina, were just returning from Mentone with a wagonload of supplies and enough barbed wire to finish fencing the forty acres south of the ranch house. Smith was not Duv's real last name and Punch knew it, but he didn't care. Smith was actually the name Duv assumed after killing a man in Fort Worth. Although the fight started out as a simple knuckle buster, when the other fella pulled a knife, Duv had no choice but to shoot him. The act was a clear case of self-defense, but the dead man's brother, a deputy sheriff, chose to ignore the facts forcing Duv to go on the run.

"Looks like Duv and Angelina are on their way back with the supplies and there's a rider with them," Luke said as he caught sight of the wagon and rider in the distance.

"Yep, looks like," Punch said while using his hand to shield his eyes from the late afternoon sun.

After returning the can of whitewash to the shelf in the barn and putting their brushes in a bucket of turpentine, Punch and Luke walked to the front of the house to see who the rider was with Duv and Angelina.

"Look what I found in Mentone," Duv shouted with a big grin.

"Well, I'll be damned!" Punch said smiling once he recognized the man on horseback. "Alvin Witherspoon."

"Hello, Punch," Alvin replied with a broad smile as he dismounted.

"I see you're still with the Rangers," Punch said after seeing the Texas Ranger badge pinned above the pocket on Alvin's faded blue shirt.

"Yeah, I reckon I just ain't thought of anything better to do," Alvin replied as he rubbed the badge with his sleeve.

"Alvin this is my son, Luke," Punch said after shaking hands with Alvin.

"Nice to meet you, Sir," Luke said as he shook Alvin's hand. "My pa has told me a lot about you."

"Hope it was all good," Alvin replied as he shook Luke's hand.

"Mostly," Luke replied, grinning.

"Well, it's nice to meet you, Luke," Alvin said after a short laugh.

"What are you doing in this neck of Texas?" Punch asked still smiling.

"Same old thing, I'm afraid. I'm after four of the worst kinda men you can imagine. They killed a man outside of Midland, raped his wife, and teenage daughter, tied 'em to their beds, and then set their house on fire."

"I'll be damned! What's this country coming to?" Punch asked shaking his head with a disgusted expression on his face. "You ain't goin' after 'em alone, are you?"

"Well, I had another ranger with me. But, we caught up with those men over by Odessa and shot it out with them. There were six of them originally. We killed two of them, but the Ranger that was with me caught a bullet in the butt when it ricocheted off a rock. Probably be awhile before he can sit a horse again. So, I left him with the doctor in Odessa and rode out after the ones that got away."

"Wasn't Chico, that took that bullet in the backside, was it?" Punch asked with a concerned look.

"No, Chico quite the Rangers a few months back. He met a gal over in Snyder... a widow woman with three kids. They got hitched and she talked him into quitin' the Rangers," Alvin said with a fond grin. "Chico made out alright, though. That gal he married... she's a real handsome woman and a real likeable sort. Besides that...her dead husband built up a real nice place before he died."

"Good for, Chico!" Punch said laughing.

"Anyway, I followed those four men as far as Mentone. Folks

in Mentone remember seeing the men passing through town. But, there was too many tracks in the road leading out of town to follow and when the road reached the Pecos...I couldn't tell if those men turned toward New Mexico or if they headed this way. So, I doubled back to Mentone and that's when I ran into Duv," Alvin said. "You ain't seen four men leading a string of horses come by here have you, Punch?"

"Nope," Punch replied, shaking his head.

"Well, I reckon those men must have gone the other direction then. They probably figure to either sell those stolen horses in Red Bluff or take 'em on into New Mexico and trade 'em to the Apaches for silver."

"You gonna keep after 'em?"

"Got to!" Alvin replied without hesitation.

"Well, it'll be dark soon. You might as well spend the night here and head out in the morning," Punch said.

"I don't want to be no bother, Punch"

"Don't be silly. You ain't no bother. Besides, Willow would give me the tongue lashing of my life, if I let you ride off without having supper and stayin' the night with us. In fact we best get on over to the house right now, so's you can tell her hello."

"I'll see to your horse, Alvin," Luke offered.

"Thanks Luke," Alvin replied.

"You got yourself a real nice place here, Punch," Alvin said as he walked with Punch to the house.

"Well, my offer still stands. I'd be glad to hire you on if you want to quit rangering."

"Thanks Punch, but I reckon I'll keep on rangering as long as I can."

When they reached the house, Punch held the screen door open for Alvin and once they were both inside, he shouted, "Willow...come see what Duv drug back from Mentone!"

"Not another stray puppy, I hope!" Willow replied as she walked into the parlor from the kitchen.

When Willow saw Alvin standing by the door, she hurried across the parlor, wrapped her arms around him, and gave him a big kiss on the cheek as she hugged him.

"Gosh, it's so good to see you! How have you been? Is Chico with you?"

"Good God, Wil... let him speak. Don't just keep shooting questions at him!" Punch laughed.

"I'm sorry! I'm just so glad to see you!" Willow said as she took a step back and looked Alvin over from head to toe.

"I been fine, Willow," Alvin said with a big smile and blushing slightly.

"You look good, but you've lost weight," Willow said still beaming with joy.

"Been chasin' too many bad men and eatin' too many meals on the trail, I reckon," Alvin replied with a sheepish look.

"You'll have supper and stay the night, won't you?"

"Okay, but just one night. I'll have to head out first thing in the morning."

"I wish I would have known you were coming. I would have cooked something special for supper."

"Didn't really know I was coming. Besides, you know how it is, Willow," Alvin said still smiling. "Any meal that ain't beans and jerky... is special!"

"You don't have to remind me of that," Willow laughed. "Well, come on into the kitchen. We can talk while I finish fixing supper."

Punch chuckled as Willow latched onto Alvin's hand and led him into the kitchen. Then he walked back outside to help Duv unload the supplies.

In the days before Punch and Willow married, Angelina had done most of the cooking and everyone including all the hired hands ate breakfast and supper together in the large kitchen at the back of the house. But after Punch married Willow and Duv married Angelina, they added a kitchen onto the bunkhouse and Angelina now prepared the meals for the hired hands in the bunkhouse and Willow now did the cooking for Punch, Luke, and her daughter, Lucy, in the kitchen of the ranch house.

"That sure was a terrific meal, Willow. And I sure thank you for it," Alvin said later after finishing off his second helping of chicken and dumplings.

"I made the dumplings," Lucy, who had just turned nine, said as she gazed at Alvin with an infatuated look.

"Yes, she did," Willow said smiling as she patted Lucy on the back.

"Well, they sure were delicious," Alvin said chuckling. "If I ate like this every day, I'd have to get a bigger saddle and a stouter horse."

"There's still a little left if you want more," Willow offered.

"Gosh no! I'm full as a tick now."

"Well, I'll put the rest in a canning jar and you can take it along with you tomorrow. At least that'll be one less meal of beans and jerky you'll have to eat."

"Thanks, Willow," Alvin said as he gave her an appreciative smile.

"Punch, why don't you and Alvin go sit on the porch and enjoy the cool night air while we get the kitchen cleaned up," Willow suggested.

"I'll be glad to help," Alvin said. "I ain't used to having anybody clean up after me."

No, you go on. I know how Punch hates pulling on that jug of his alone," Willow said staring at Punch.

"Man gets mighty thirsty working out in that heat all day," Punch said grinning as he got up from the table.

"Just a minute, young man," Willow said quickly as Luke started to follow Punch and Alvin out of the kitchen."

"Ohhhh Willow, I'm nearly sixteen. I'm too old to be doin' women's work in the kitchen. Can't I go outside with pa and Ranger Witherspoon?"

"That's Aunt Willow to you, mister," Willow said in a stern voice, but with an amused smile. "And no... you can't go with your pa and Alvin until we get this kitchen cleaned up. But...since you're nearly sixteen! I'll let you choose whether you wash or dry."

Punch and Alvin chuckled as they continued toward the front porch. When they reached the front door, Punch paused long enough to open the top of the bench on the hall tree and after pulling out a gallon sized jug of whiskey, he closed the bench top and held the screen door open for Alvin. Once they were both on the porch, they sat down in two of the rockers that lined the wall on both sides of the door.

"After you my friend," Punch said as he pulled the cork out of the jug and offered it to Alvin.

"That's not bad," Alvin said after taking a large swallow.

"Yep, I think it's even better than most of the stuff that comes in the bottles with the fancy labels. And the best part is…it costs half as much," Punch said after taking a healthy sample.

"It ain't your making by chance?"

"No, I ain't got the time nor the talent to make anything this good."

"How'd you come by it?"

"Oh, there's and old Mexican man that comes by here about once a month with a donkey pulling a two wheeled cart full of the stuff. I used to buy two jugs every time he come by. But lately, I've cut back to just one."

"Willow have anything to do with that?" Alvin asked with a slight chuckle as he held out his hand for the jug.

"Partially…she keeps reminding me that Luke is growing up and I need to set a good example for him. Mind you, I don't think there's anything wrong with taking a snort or two now and then. My daddy did it and he never tried to hide it. And I intend to follow his example. But after two or three …or maybe four depending on the company you're with," Punch chuckled. "Anyway... after a few snorts, it's time to put a cork in it."

"You said partially…what was the other part that made you cut back?" Alvin asked after taking another swallow and offering the jug back to Punch.

"Well, I always emptied one jug before I started in on the other. One night I took the last swallow out of one jug and I went to get the other. I uncorked it and I lifted it up just a little expecting it to be full and then I lifted it a little more and then I lifted it a little more. And it suddenly dawned on me that the jug wasn't full. So, I swished it around a bit and decided it was about one third empty. Well, I had a talk with young Mister Luke and he fessed up."

"At least he owned up to it," Alvin said after a short laugh.

"Yeah, and I was proud of him for it. Of course I didn't let on I was proud of him. But Luke's always been that way...he's always been honest even when he's done wrong."

"He's a fine young man," Alvin said. "How old were you the first time you took a drink, Punch?" Alvin asked after another short laugh.

"Hell, I think I was a year or two younger than Luke when my brother and I got into a bottle of my daddy's best bourbon."

"Did you get caught?"

"Yep, wasn't no hiding it. Neither one of us could stand up without holding on to something and we could barely talk."

"What did your pa do? Give you a licking?"

"Nope, he knew neither one of us would feel a thing...drunk as we were. So, he marched us out to the kitchen and sat us down at the table. Then he sat another bottle on the table and told us to help ourselves. Boy we really thought we was special. Then he proceeded to cook up a big pot of greasy pork chili. Just the smell of it made our stomachs go to twitching. When it was done, he served each of us a big bowl of the fowl smelling stuff and he told us we had to eat every bit of it. Once we started eating it… it came out of both ends just as fast as we spooned it in."

Both Punch and Alvin laughed and after they each had one more drink, Punch put the cork in the jug and sat it on the porch next to his chair.

"So, tell me about these men you're after, Alvin."

"They're a bad lot, Punch. They're the worst kind of men I've ever heard of. They're as evil as Lucifer himself. They been killing folks and violating women, even young girls, all the way across Texas. The worst of the lot is a man named Warren Henderson. He's the leader of the bunch. From what I understand, he was a Confederate Captain during the war. He was wounded and captured by the Yankees at the battle of Look Out Mountain. Got a big scar across his face and he wears a patch over his left eye. He spent two years in the Delaware Prison Camp which I reckon is one of the reasons he's the way he is. I was told he killed a man with his bare hands over a loaf of moldy bread when he was in that prison camp. Then he ripped the man's stomach open with his belt buckle and ate the man's liver."

"My god! He sounds more like a wild animal than a man!"

"Yeah and the men he's with ain't much better. One of them is a man named, Bartholomew Bond. He was a sergeant in Henderson's company and he was captured at the same time. Before the war, he made his living hunting runaway slaves. Rumor has it he fathered a half dozen kids with different Negro women. The third man is a half breed that calls himself Billy Wolf. He was serving time in Huntsville for cuttin' up a whore. He and those other two men that we killed in that shootout near Odessa... killed a guard and escaped from a work detail about two months ago. I don't know too much about the fourth man. He's a young fella, probably not more than nineteen or twenty. I'm not sure how long ago he joined up with Henderson and Bond, but I know he was in on the killing and raping of that woman and her fourteen year old daughter."

"You still set on going after em alone?"

"I got to, Punch. If I wait around for help to come, they'll likely cross over into the New Mexico Territory and there ain't no other lawmen between here and the state line."

"Well, I reckon I best go with you then," Punch said in a solemn voice.

"I couldn't ask you to do that, Punch."

"You didn't ask... I offered," Punch said with a steadfast look. "It's the least I can do after all you did for me and Willow when our cattle was rustled."

"I was just doin' my job, Punch."

"Maybe so, but I'd like to return the favor. And I reckon it's my job as a Texan to see to it that these animals are stopped and brought to justice."

"What will Willow say?"

"What would any wife say? But in her heart, she'll know I'm doing the right thing."

"Besides, remember how you used to always bring up odds. Well, two against four is a whole lot better than one against four!"

"But what about the ranch? I know it's nearly time for the

spring roundup and branding."

"Duv, Luke, and the rest of my men can take care of things while I'm gone."

"Well, I reckon I got no real good argument then, Punch. Except maybe, to remind you that you got Willow, and Luke, and Lucy to think about."

"I've already thought about all of them and my mind's made up."

"Well Punch, if there's no changing your mind…you know I'd surely welcome the help. I just hope it don't cause Willow to have bad feelings toward me."

"Don't you worry about Willow. Like I said, it was my idea not yours. But, don't mention anything about it to her. I'd like to tell her myself when we're alone."

Willow, Luke, and Lucy joined Alvin and Punch on the front porch a few minutes later and nothing more was said about the men Alvin was chasing. The conversation turned instead to the changing times and things that Alvin had seen in his travels around Texas. By the time Alvin ran out of things to say, it was already past everyone's normal bedtime. So, after they all said goodnight, they went to their respective rooms for what they hoped would be a good night's sleep.

Punch laid in bed silently watching Willow brush her long brown hair as he tried to think about the best way to tell her about his decision to go with Alvin. Once she joined him in bed, Punch blew out the kerosene lantern by the bed and put his arm around Willow as she laid her head on his shoulder.

"It sure was nice seeing Alvin again after two years," Willow said smiling. "I just wish he would do like Chico… settle down and leave the Rangers. It troubles me to know that he's wasting his whole life chasing desperados and killers."

"Well as matter of fact, it troubles me too. And I don't like the fact that he's often alone when he's going after killers and men of despicable character. He didn't mention it to you because he's not the type to bring up such things, but he's going after four men tomorrow that are guilty of murder and things too horrible to talk about."

"Is he going alone?"

"Well, he was...but I've decided to lend him a hand."

"No Punch! Please, I beg you...don't go," Willow said as she rolled over on his chest and looked into his eyes.

"I don't want to go, Wil...but it's the right thing to do. I owe him a lot for what he did when our cattle were taken. We both do...and now he could use my help and I feel like I owe it to him to return the favor."

"Did Alvin ask for your help?"

"No, he would never do that. In fact, he tried to talk me out of going. But these four men he's after...they're animals...dangerous animals...they think nothing of killing men, raping women, and even burning folks alive."

"Couldn't Alvin send for help?"

"There's no time, Wil. Those men are headed for the New Mexico Territory and by the time help arrived... they would already be across the state line. So, I gotta do it, Wil. I gotta help Alvin."

"I guess so," Willow said as tears started to run down her cheeks. "Sometimes you make me wish I had fallen in love with a man that could just look the other way when there was trouble."

"Well, it's not like we just met, Wil. We've known each other since we were kids. So, you should know what to expect from me by now."

"Yes, I know. I'm not surprised by your decision. But, it doesn't keep me from wishing you would learn to look the other way."

"Well, it's just not what I do, Wil."

"I know and I love you for it," Willow said as she sat up and pulled off her nightgown. "Just promise me you'll be careful and come back to me."

Chapter Two

    The two bells on the old wind up alarm clock by the bed startled Punch out of a sound sleep. He quickly grabbed the clock and fumbled with the lever to turn off the obnoxious clanking.
    "What time is it?" Willow asked after a drawn out yawn.
    "Five thirty," Punch replied as he struck a match and lit the kerosene lamp on the night table.
    "Alright, if you'll start a fire in the kitchen stove, I'll be out directly to fix breakfast."
    After kissing Willow good morning, Punch got out of bed, dressed, and as he passed the spare bedroom on his way to the kitchen, he could hear Alvin rustling about. Punch put several pieces of kindling in the stove from the wood box and once the fire was lit, he pumped water into the large coffee pot, added some fresh grinds, and Willow walked into the kitchen just as Punch was putting the coffee pot on the stove. While Willow prepared breakfast, Punch returned to the bedroom and after pulling his oversized saddlebags and bedroll from under the bed, he proceeded to pack for a few days on the trail.
    He could smell the bacon frying and coffee brewing the instant he stepped back into the hallway. Alvin was sitting at the large pine table, drinking coffee, when Punch returned to the kitchen.
    "Mornin', Punch"
    "Mornin', Alvin," Punch replied as he walked to the stove for some coffee.
    "I guess you ain't changed your mind about going with me."
    "Did you really expect him to?" Willow asked glancing at Alvin from the stove.
    "Well, I thought just maybe... you might have talked him out of it," Alvin said with a slightly timid look.
    "I'd have better luck talking a mule out of something," Willow said after a soft laugh. "Besides do you really think I would even try to change his mind?"
    "Well, I just want you to know it weren't my idea for Punch to go with me. So, I hope you don't have no bad feelings toward me, Willow."

"Of course not," Willow said with a sincere look. "I don't like the thought of either of you going out after those men. But, I know it has to be done and I know it's the right thing to do."

As soon as Punch and Alvin finished their breakfasts, they went to the barn to saddle their horses while Willow gathered an assortment of food and supplies from the kitchen pantry.

"We ain't going for a month, Wil!" Punch said chuckling when he and Alvin returned to the kitchen and saw the assortment of supplies that Willow had piled on the table.

"I know, but there's no sense starving yourselves," Willow replied.

"No, but we ain't taking a wagon," Punch laughed. "We can only take what we can put in our saddlebags."

As a compromise, in addition to some jerky and the things they put in their saddlebags, Punch put an assortment of tins, some flour, dried beans, coffee, a loaf of bread, and a small wheel of cheese in an empty flour sack.

"Well, I guess we best hit the trail," Punch said as he finished tying a string around the flour sack.

"It sure was good to see you, Willow. I appreciate the meals and the soft bed to sleep in. You got a real nice place here. Tell Lucy I said good-bye and Luke, too," Alvin said as he fidgeted with his hat.

"You're welcome back anytime," Willow said with a warm smile as she put her arms around Alvin, hugged him, and kissed him on the cheek. "You be careful and take care of yourself."

"Thanks, I will," Alvin said blushing.

"I'll be out directly, Alvin," Punch said as he held the flour sack out to Alvin.

Once they were alone, Punch and Willow embraced, kissed a long kiss, and then they just held each other tightly. Punch could feel Willows tears on his cheek as he said softly, "Don't worry we'll be fine."

"I love you, Peyote Masters."

"I love you too, Willow. You know that," Punch said.

They kissed again and after another firm embrace, Punch said, "Tell Lucy and Luke good-bye for me."

"When do you think you'll be back?"

"The state line is only about forty five or fifty miles away. So, I imagine I'll be back in four or five days at the most. If for some reason I'm gonna be gone longer, I'll get word to you."

Punch and Willow kissed one more time and then Punch joined Alvin outside. They exchanged waves as Punch and Alvin rode off at a gentle trot. When they reached a slight rise in the road, Punch looked back and gave Willow one last wave before disappearing over the rise.

When Punch and Alvin were about two miles past where the road from Mentone intersected with the road that paralleled the river, they spotted several buzzards a short distance ahead effortlessly gliding around in circles.

"Must be something dead up ahead," Alvin said.

"Yeah, I just hope it's something and not somebody," Punch replied with a concerned look. "There's a young Mexican couple that lives just across the river up ahead."

"Maybe they got a cow that died," Alvin said trying to be optimistic, but secretly sharing Punch's concern.

"No, they got no cattle. They raise goats and I doubt if one died Miguel would leave it for the buzzards," Punch said as he nudged his horse with his spurs to hasten its pace.

Punch and Alvin galloped a short distance up the road until they reached the shallow river crossing where the road to the Ortez adobe intersected with the main road. Their troubled expressions intensified as they noticed the multitude of horse prints in the wet sand along the river bank and as they crossed the river, the slight breeze brought the stench of death to their nostrils. Once they were across the river, both men put their horses into a gallop and as they came within fifty yards of the adobe and saw the mass of buzzards on the ground near the goat pen, Punch pulled his pistol and fired a shot into the air. The black feathered cloak that shrouded Miguel's body suddenly lifted and the sky filled with the black birds of death, shrieking, and rapidly flapping their wings to join those that were still circling overhead.

Punch and Alvin slowed their horses as they realized they were too late to be of any help to Miguel. When they reached the goat pen, they pulled their bandanas up over their noses and dismounted. Their horses danced nervously as they saw and smelled the body. Shreds of flesh along with bits of torn and bloody clothing littered the blood stained sand. The buzzards and coyotes had stripped the flesh from the entire back of Miguel's body exposing his backbone and part of his hip and femurs.

Both Alvin and Punch turned away and quickly lifted their bandanas as they felt their breakfast coming up.

"Probably be best to tie our horses upwind until we get him buried," Punch said after emptying his stomach. "I don't guess there's any question that this is the work of those four men we're after,"

"No, it's them alright. You can see where they tied the string of stolen horses over there by that shed," Alvin said after spitting several times trying to get the vile taste of vomit out of his mouth.

"Miguel had a grey stallion and a sorrel mare. I reckon that's what those men were after and the reason they shot Miguel," Punch said as he looked toward the pasture and saw only a handful of goats."

"Did you say there was a young couple living here?"

"I'm afraid so," Punch said. "Miguel and Maria Ortez...and they had a new baby boy, too. I reckon we'll probably find their bodies inside the adobe."

"Maybe not," Alvin said pointing toward the side of the adobe where a buzzard had just landed.

"Damned buzzards!" Punch said with anger building in his eyes as he handed Alvin the reins to his horse.

Punch pulled his pistol as he continued walking toward the buzzard that was perched on what he was about to discover was Maria's remains.

The buzzard raised its hideous red head with a piece of intestines dangling from its beak and squawked defiantly at Punch with its wings outstretched. Punch cursed at the buzzard, raised his pistol, and pulled the trigger. A puff of feathers flew into the air as Punch's bullet hit the buzzard throwing it back a few feet.

When Punch got a good look of Maria's naked, mutilated body with her empty eye sockets staring up at the sky, he doubled over, gaging, and convulsing with the dry heaves.

"You alright, Punch?" Alvin shouted

"Yeah, it's Maria alright. Check inside for the baby will you?" Punch said as he stood upright holding his trembling stomach.

Alvin went inside the adobe and Punch quickly wiped the tears that had suddenly started to streak down his cheeks.

"No sign of any baby, Punch. There's a crib by the bed, but it's empty," Alvin shouted as he walked back out of the adobe.

"Okay, see if you can find a shovel and I'll have a look around out here for the baby. Looks like Maria was busy working on planting a garden before they killed her. She probably had the baby outside with her."

It didn't take Punch long to find the empty overturned basket on the north side of the adobe and when he found the small blanket covered in dried blood and saw the coyote prints in the dirt, he knew there was no reason to keep looking.

"Find anything, Punch?" Alvin shouted as he walked out of the shed by the goat pen carrying a shovel.

"Found enough to tell me the baby's dead and there's no reason to keep looking," Punch shouted back, again drying his eyes.

"What do you mean, Punch?" Alvin asked.

"Looks like the coyotes drug him off," Punch said wiping his eyes to fight back more tears. "And I hate to say it...but there's no sense wasting time looking for a body...cause there ain't gonna be enough left to bury by the time the coyotes are finished with him. So, there's no sense wasting time looking."

"Well, I guess we might as well get busy burying Maria and Miguel then before the sun gets any higher," Alvin said shaking his head with a disgusted look and sad eyes.

"I want to catch these bastards, Alvin," Punch said practically trembling with anger. "I don't care if I have to chase 'em all the way to California. I mean to catch 'em."

"I want to catch 'em too, Punch."

"Then you best get after 'em, Alvin. I'll stay here to bury Miguel and Maria. Once I'm done here, I'll catch up to you."

"I hate to leave you here to deal with this alone, Punch."

"Well, the best thing you can do for Miguel, Maria...and their baby boy, now... is to go after the bastards that did this. If we're lucky, they'll camp one more time before they reach Red Bluff."

"I guess you're right, Punch. If I come across their camp before you catch up to me, I'll double back a ways and wait for you. Then come sunrise, we'll get the drop on em."

"You aim to bring 'em in alive?"

"I've learned a lot of things since I first joined the Rangers, Punch. A few years ago, I would have done my best to bring these men in alive ...even after what they've done. But now... I don't think so, Punch. The nearest judge is all the way back in Pecos. And there's no question about what went on here...and it ain't their first time. All four of these men are guilty of rape, murder, horse thievery, and God knows what else. So, I mean to kill 'em outright or hang 'em on the spot," Alvin said with no hint of reluctance.

"Well, you'll get no argument from me," Punch said in a deliberate tone.

"Alright Punch, I'll be waitin' for you," Alvin said as he handed Punch the shovel.

Once Alvin was mounted and on his way, Punch went inside of the adobe for two blankets to wrap the bodies in and after wrapping the bodies, he proceeded to dig a hole large enough for both bodies. Punch had just finished placing Miguel's remains in the grave and was about to do the same with Maria's when he stopped and walked to the north side of the adobe and returned with the small blanket that the baby had been swaddled in. After rolling up the small blanket, he peeled back the blanket wrapped around Maria just enough to expose her arms and then he placed the small rolled up blanket in her arms. Tears again rolled down his cheeks as he again wrapped the blanket around Maria and lowered her body into the grave beside her dead husband. Once the grave was filled in with dirt, Punch walked to the shed by the goat pen and used the shovel to pry a plank from the side of the shed. He spent several minutes carving *Miguel Ortez* and *Maria Ortez* on the plank and then added the words *Baby Ortez* below Maria's name. After placing the marker on the grave, he stood with his hat in hand trying to think of something to say over the graves, but his mind was full of dark thoughts and revenge. So, after a few minutes of silence he simply said, "Rest in peace Miguel, Maria, and Baby Ortez," then as he put on his hat and started walking toward his horse he muttered, "I'll get these bastards for you."

As the sun began to set, the Warren Henderson, Bartholomew Bond, his brother Ted and the half breed named Billy Medina stopped to set up camp in a dry ravine next to the road about eight miles from Red Bluff. After watering the horses by the river, the four men unsaddled them and rigged up a picket line to keep their mounts and the string of eight additional horses from wandering off.

"Hey Billy," the Captain said as the four men were carrying their saddles to the spot where they planned on bedding down. "How about filling up all of the canteens while the rest of us see what we can scrounge up to make a fire?"

Although the request seemed innocent enough, Billy had a suspicious streak that made him question the motive behind even the simplest requests or actions. So rather than respond immediately, he glanced at Bart and then Ted before fixing his eyes on the captain.

"How about it, Billy?" the captain repeated.

"Okay Warren," Billy replied glancing at Bart and Ted again.

Even though Billy had lived among the white man for more years than he had spent with the Kiowa, he still distrusted all white men and he hated them almost as much as he hated Indians. His mother was only sixteen when she became a captive. She and her mother were taken when a Kiowa war party raided their family ranch in the Texas panhandle. Her mother was later killed after being raped by most of the braves on the raid and Billy's mother would have met the same fate, had it not been for the fact that a Kiowa War Chief named Grey Wolf claimed her as his own and later made her his third wife. Grey Wolf's other wives, both of whom were full blooded Kiowa, were not happy about the marriage. And as a result, she was shunned by the other wives and regularly subjected to harsh treatment which only got worse once Billy was born. Billy was nine when a detachment of U.S. Cavalry attacked the Kiowa village, and once the fighting was over, Billy and his mother were taken to Amarillo. But the humiliation and treatment they received from the good citizens of Amarillo was not much better than the treatment they had received from the Kiowa. Billy's mother eventually turned to prostitution in order to put food on the table and Billy got a job in the same saloon, sweeping the floor, cleaning spittoons, and doing whatever else he was told. His mother died of an undetermined venereal disease when Billy was thirteen and Billy found himself living on the streets soon thereafter. By the time Billy was sixteen, he had grown to hate whites just as much as he hated red men and he trusted no one.

The captain pretended to gather dried sage and grass, but his eyes never left Billy until he disappeared in the thick brush that hugged the banks of the river. At which time, the captain tossed his hand full of grass and dried sage on the ground and motioned to the sergeant to join him by their saddles.

"What's up, Captain?" Bart asked when he reached the saddles.

"I think it's time to dissolve our partnership with the half breed," the captain said as he pulled his Winchester from the saddle scabbard.

"How come?" Bart asked looking somewhat surprised.

"What do we need him for? We'll be in New Mexico by this time tomorrow and after that shoot out with those Rangers, I doubt we're being followed. So, why should we split the money we get for the horses four ways? Hell, we did most of the work anyway. And besides that... I don't trust him."

"Fine by me, Captain," the sergeant said shrugging his shoulders. "How do you want to do it?"

"I say we get our rifles and let him have it right now while he's down at the river filling the canteens."

The sergeant pulled his rifle and then the two men hurried to the edge of the brush along the bank of the river leaving Ted, who had no idea what was about to happen, gathering tinder for the fire. Billy had just finished filling the four canteens when he heard the bushes behind him rustling. He stood up quickly reaching for his pistol as he turned around, only to be knocked over backwards when the bullet tore into his shoulder. He struggled to his feet and started running across the river which was barely above his ankles.

A second bullet slammed into his back throwing him face first into the water. He lifted his head above the water gasping for air and started crawling toward the sand bar just ahead of him. Another shot rang out and he collapsed on the sand bar as the bullet hit him in the back of the head spraying the sand with blood and brains.

"I thought the son of a bitch was never gonna die," the Captain said laughing as he as he worked the lever on his Winchester ejecting the spent cartridge."

"What the hell's all the shooting about?" Ted shouted as he ran toward the two men with his pistol in hand.

"Shot us an *Injun,*" his brother, the sergeant, replied laughing. "First one I ever killed. Felt kinda good, too!"

"I'm not sure killing a half breed qualifies as killing an *Injun*, Bart," the Captain said as he slapped Bart on the back and continued laughing.

"What did Billy, do?" Ted asked with a curious look, but with no hint of genuine concern.

"Nothing, we just decided we didn't need him anymore," the captain replied in a matter of fact voice.

"What do you care, anyhow? Once we sell the horses...without Billy...it just leaves a bigger share for the rest of us," Bart added.

"Speaking of which, I'm gonna ride on into Red Bluff and look things over." the captain said.

"Why don't we all go?" Bart asked.

"No, I want you and Ted to stay here with the horses while I go scout things out and make sure there's no telegraph in Red Bluff. If there is, the good citizens of Red Bluff are likely to know we're coming and they might be waiting to gun us down."

Alvin was still a couple miles away from where the captain and his gang stopped to camp when he heard the three muffled shots. He pulled his horse to a stop and stared in the direction of the shots, as he wondered about their purpose.

"Hope they ain't doin' more killing!" Alvin thought out loud as he continued staring in the distance, listening for more shots.

After listening for a few additional minutes and hearing no more shots, Alvin gently spurred his horse and continued loping toward the setting sun. After continuing a short distance, Alvin spotted a thin line of smoke against the now crimson sky and again reined his horse to a stop. He pulled the binoculars from his saddlebags and started scanning the road and prairie ahead hoping to spot the source of the smoke which he was certain was a campfire. But, the rolling terrain dotted with sage brush, cactus, and tall yucca prevented him from seeing anything except for the thin line of smoke that continued rising against the back drop of pink clouds.

    Alvin put the binocular strap around his neck, and pulled his Winchester as he dismounted. Then he continued on foot, leading his horse, until he estimated that the smoke was about a mile away. He crouched down by the side of the road and again used his binoculars to scan the terrain ahead. After seeing nothing, Alvin led his horse to the river. While his horse drank, Alvin scooped several handfuls of water into his mouth and then splashed some in his face. Once his horse was well watered, Alvin led the horse up the bank and tied it to a stout willow bush where it was still visible from the road. Then he loosened the cinch on the saddle and pulled some jerky from his saddlebags. While the horse grazed on the grass at the base of the bush and stripped the tender, narrow leaves from the bush's slender branches, Alvin sat on the ground nearby chewing on his jerky and occasionally raising his binoculars to look back down the road hoping to see Punch riding his way. As the shades of red and pink disappeared form the clouds and the last rays of daylight gave into darkness, Alvin removed his spurs and stuffed them along with the binoculars in his saddlebags. Then after taking off his gun belt, he buckled it with the two colt pistols and sheath knife still in place and looped it over the saddle horn. What remained of the moon, which had been full three nights earlier, was just making an appearance above the eastern horizon when Alvin removed his hat and placed it on top of his gun belt, picked up his rifle, and again started down the road in the direction of the smoke. As he walked, Alvin bent over slightly at the waist and moved to the side of the road to take advantage of the shadows cast by the sagebrush hugging the road. The slight breeze from the west brought with it the campfire smell and after traveling about half a mile further, Alvin started to hear voices and laughter. He dropped to his knees and crouched in the shadows by the side of the road, listening to the voices. A surge of light suddenly erupted in the distance and embers shot into the air as the sergeant tossed a handful of dried sage onto the dwindling fire. Determined to get a closer look, Alvin left the road and continued toward the light cautiously making his way through the sagebrush and yucca. When he was finally close enough to see the campfire and the two men by it, he laid down on his belly. His mouth was dry and he could hear his heart pounding as he lay there watching Bart and his brother talking, laughing, and passing a bottle back and forth between them. Alvin's strained eyes searched the outer rim of light for Billy and the captain, but saw nothing. When his eyes reached the horses and Alvin noticed the gray stallion was not among them, he shifted his attention to the saddles he had seen earlier near the campfire. "Only three saddles," he thought to himself. Then he noticed that one of the saddles still had the bedroll tied behind the cantle and his heart began pounding louder as he wondered if Billy or the captain might be somewhere out in the darkness, perhaps even near where he was lying, standing guard or circling the campsite on foot like a sentry.

    Suddenly Alvin heard an all too familiar sound a few feet from his left ear. It was the sound of a rattlesnake about to strike. Alvin knew that even the slightest twitch might cause the serpent to strike. So, his eyes searched the dark ground and shadows to his left while his body remained frozen. His eyes saw nothing, but the buzzing in his ear told him the snake was very close and Alvin knew that a bite to his face or neck would be fatal. Alvin decided his best option would be to quickly roll to the right and hope that the move would put him out of the snakes reach. So after mentally counting to three, he quickly rolled to his right. The instant he moved he felt a sharp stinging sensation in his left hand and he knew he had been bitten. He rolled again before looking back and caught just a glimpse of the snake in the moonlight. Alvin pulled the bandanna from around his neck and used his teeth to help tie it around his wrist. He could feel his hand already beginning to swell and the pain intensifying as he broke a branch off of a nearby sage and stuck it through the loop, twisting it to cut off the flow of blood to and from his hand. He knew he was in trouble, so Alvin got to his feet, but remained crouched over being careful not to release the tourniquet around his left wrist. He tried to steady his breathing and slow his heartbeat as he started making his way back to his horse. Once he was sure he could not be seen by the men at the campfire, he headed straight to the road and hastened his pace. In the distance he saw what he thought was the silhouette of another horse next to his.

"Is that you, Punch?" Alvin asked in a loud whisper once he was a short distance from the horses.

"You better hope it's me," Punch said chuckling.

"I'm in trouble, Punch! I been snake bit!"

"Let's take a look," Punch said as he stepped out into the moonlight and rushed toward Alvin.

Punch struck a match on his boot and held it so he could see Alvin's hand which was swollen to the point that it resembled a baseball mitt of the period.

"Looks like it got you in the finger," Punch said as he spotted the two telltale puncture marks on his left index finger just ahead of the knuckle.

"I guess I was lucky," Alvin said with a short laugh.

"Don't be so sure," Punch said in a concerned tone as he shook out the match. "The poison has already spread throughout your whole hand and if we don't get it out, you're liable to loose that hand."

Punch got a candle out of his saddlebag and after lighting it, he cut a willow branch for Alvin to bite on if the pain became unbearable. After making some adjustments to the tourniquet, Punch passed the blade of his knife through the candle flame a few times to sterilize it and once the blade cooled, he handed Alvin the willow stick to bight down on and made a series of cuts across the back of Alvin's hand hopping to draw out some of the venom.

"This ain't gonna work Alvin," Punch said after seeing that Alvin's finger had turned completely black. We gotta cut that finger off otherwise you're liable to lose your whole hand and maybe even your arm...that is if you live."

"The hell you say! You can't be serious!" Alvin said with a shocked look after spitting out the willow stick.

"I'm afraid so, Alvin. We got no choice. The venom has already started to kill all the tissue in that finger."

Once Alvin agreed, little more was said between Alvin and Punch. Punch untied Alvin's bedroll from his saddle and after rolling it out, Alvin sat on it holding his left hand while Punch returned to the bushes in search of a thick willow branch to use as a chopping block. After breaking off the thickest branch he could find, he turned his attention to the ground and found a stone large enough to use as a hammer to drive his knife blade through the bone of Alvin's finger. Then he got a clean bandanna out of his saddlebag, doused Alvin's hand with water from his canteen, and used the candle flame to again sterilize his knife.

"Ready, Alvin?" Punch asked trying to look calm and unruffled.

"I reckon so" Alvin replied in a shaky voice.

"Okay, lie down on your back and bite down hard," Punch said handing Alvin the willow stick.

"I could sure use some whiskey from that jug you keep in the hall tree about now," Alvin said trying to manage a smile.

"We both could," Punch replied.

Alvin laid down and after putting the stick in his mouth, he turned away as tears started to build in his eyes. His right hand trembled and he could feel his knees doing the same as Punch stretched out his left hand and placed the blackened finger across the large willow branch. Punch moved the candle closer to Alvin's outstretched hand and that's all Alvin remembered until a few hours later when he woke up and felt the throbbing in his left hand.

It was still dark and the moon was directly overhead. Alvin reached across with his right hand and felt the bandanna wrapped around his left hand.

"How do you feel?" Punch asked when he detected Alvin's movement."

"How do you think I feel?"

"Fair enough, I guess it was a stupid question," Punch said in what sounded like an optimistic tone. "Can you move your fingers? Barely, but they're awful tight and the rest of my hand feels like there's somebody inside it pounding on a drum."

"Well, that throbbing and tightness should start to go away once the swelling goes down."

"That the neckerchief you wrapped it in feels kinda sticky."

"Well, I put a hot blade to the blood veins to stop the bleeding, but I left the wound open to let it drain. I got a needle and thread in my saddlebag. Once the sun comes up and I can see better, I'll stitch it up. In the meantime, we'll just keep washing it off and try to keep it clean."

"I sure am sorry about this, Punch. I'm afraid I won't be much help to you now."

"Not your fault, Alvin. You were just in the wrong place at the wrong time. Anyway, I assume you found their camp."

"Yeah, it's about a mile further up the way. They're camped in a shallow draw on the south side of the road. I only actually saw two of 'em in camp. I never saw Henderson or Billy Wolf and that grey stallion you mentioned; the one you said belonged to Miguel Ortez... it was gone. But, I counted three saddles on the ground by the fire. So, I figured one of 'em might have been away from the fire standing guard on foot and the other one could be mounted or one of 'em might have rode on into Red Bluff.

"Henderson...he the one with the patch?"

"Yep."

"If he's the leader of the bunch, he might have gone on into Red Bluff to try to line up a buyer for that string of stolen horses they got."

"Yeah, that's kinda what I thought, too."

"Well, I guess we'll find out once the sun comes up," Punch said reaching for the canteen. "You thirsty?"

"Yeah, I'll take some whiskey if you got it."

"I wish I did," Punch replied as he uncorked the canteen and held it out to Alvin.

Chapter Three

Alvin had again dozed off and was sleeping soundly. He woke with a sudden jerk when Punch placed the wet bandanna back on his forehead after wetting with water from his canteen.

"You feel like you're still running a fever, Alvin." Punch said.

"I feel kinda sick to my stomach and my muscles ache all over, too," Alvin replied.

"Well, rattlesnake bites are known to make folks pretty sick. But, it should pass after a day or so," Punch said. "Anyway, looks like the swelling is starting to go down in your hand. How's the pain?"

"About the same."

"You gonna be alright by yourself for a few hours? I'm fixin' to head on over to where those men are camped. I want to be set up before the sun rises."

"I'll be fine, Punch. Sorry I can't give you a hand," Alvin replied.

"Well, that's just the way the cards fell," Punch said in a matter of fact tone. "Thought, I'd borrow one of your pistols if you don't mind. Might come in handy and keep me from having to reload if things don't go well from the start."

"Help yourself. I doubt I'll even be able to hold a pistol in my left hand anymore," Alvin replied in a depressed voice.

"Well, you might trade in one of those full sized Colts of yours for a smaller pistol. Maybe get yourself one of those belly guns that you can hide out. Probably come in pretty handy for a man in your profession. Anyway, I best get going. I'll be back as soon as I can."

"Watch out for snakes!" Alvin said with a weak smile.

"I will and if I see that one that bit you, I'll kill it and bring it back so's you can have the satisfaction of eating it!" Punch said smiling back.

After stuffing one of Alvin's pistols in his waist band, Punch laid the other one on the ground within easy reach of Alvin and then he headed up the road. The moon was low in the western sky, but the fading moonlight was still enough that Punch could make out Alvin's boot prints in the sandy soil. And even though all that remained of the campfire was some smoldering embers, Punch could still smell it lingering in the air. When Punch came to the spot where Alvin's footprints left the road, Punch followed them, but they quickly disappeared in shadows of the sage brush, so Punch began picking his own way through the sage, yucca, and cactus. Punch stopped and crouched behind a cluster of sage as he spotted what he thought were the horses and when he heard one snort and another whinny softly, he knew that he had found the camp. Punch started to lie down in the sand, but quickly stopped and cautiously poked around at the bases of the surrounding sage brush with the barrel of his rifle. After hearing nothing, he chuckled softly to himself and laid down on his stomach.

    About an hour later, rays of sunlight began to overpower the soft glow of the moon which was still visible just above the western horizon. As the sounds of birds chirping and things rustling in the morning breeze replaced the sounds of the night, Punch slowly raised his head above the sage to get a better idea of where he was in relation to the men's camp He could see the horses ahead and slightly to his left, but he was too far away to see into the dry wash where the men were camped and still sleeping. Punch rolled onto his left side, so he could get at Alvin's Colt that was still tucked in his belt. Then he shifted his gun belt until the holster was in the small of his back and stuck Alvin's pistol in his belt next to the holster where it would be out of the way, but accessible. While he was on his side, he caught a glimpse of movement in the sky off to his right. He turned his head and realized it was buzzards circling above the river. After watching the birds of death, effortlessly riding the wind for a few seconds, Punch cradled the Winchester in his arms and started crawling on his belly toward the ravine. A small covey of quail suddenly flushed a few yards ahead of him taking away his breath and momentarily stopping his heart. Punch let out a long sigh and inaudible chuckle, then he continued crawling at a desert tortoise's pace until he was close enough to the wash to see the two bedrolls with men still asleep inside. When he noticed the third saddle with the bedroll still tied behind the cantle, he tried to make sense of it as his eyes searched for the saddle's owner. He glanced at the picket line where the horses were tied; looking for the grey stallion and saw it was still missing. As he turned his attention back to the bedrolls, he noticed one of the men starting to stir. A moment later arms appeared stretching toward the sky and then the bedroll fell to the man's waist as Bartholomew Bond sat up yawning. He picked up a bottle that was at the side of his bedroll and held it up hoping to find enough for one last swallow and then cursed as he flung the empty bottle aside. After rubbing his stiff neck, he threw back the bedroll and reached for his boots that were next to his saddle, which at the time, was being used as a pillow. After turning the boots upside down to ensure there were no unwanted tenants inside, Bart pulled on his boots and walked a few steps away from his bedroll to empty his bladder. After relieving himself, he walked to the other bed roll and nudged the sleeping inhabitant with his boots.

"Get up, Ted!" he said loudly.

Ted reluctantly raised his head, squinting to block the bright sunlight. Then he sat up and stretched as he let out a loud drawn out yawn.

"Snappy outfit," Ted laughed as he looked at Bart who was gathering tinder wearing only his faded red long johns and black stove pipe boots.

"Shut up and help me gather some wood for the fire. My heads killin' me and I need a cup of coffee."

"What's the matter, big brother, can't hold you liquor?" Ted replied as he slithered out of his bedroll.

Punch slowly cracked the action on his Winchester just enough to make sure there was a cartridge in the chamber, closed it, and slowly cocked the hammer. He took aim at Ted who had just finished pulling on his pants and was now standing on his bedroll. Punch took a breath and slowly let it out as his trigger finger started to tighten, but before the rifle made a sound, his finger stopped and he relaxed his hand. Although, Punch knew the men needed and deserved to be killed, shooting two unsuspecting, unarmed men suddenly didn't seem like the proper thing to do. So after giving it some thought, Punch decided that he would wait until the two men were side by side, perhaps by the fire, with their hands occupied holding a cup of hot coffee, and then he would show himself and get the drop on them.

Bart started a fire and after filling the coffee pot with water from his canteen, he added a handful of coffee grinds, and placed the pot at the edge of the fire. Ted in the meantime, finished dressing and strapped on his gun belt before joining his brother by the fire. When Bart filled a cup with coffee and handed it to Ted. Punch got to his knees, but remained hidden as Bart filled another cup for himself. When Bart raised the cup to his lips, Punch stood up quickly, bringing his Winchester up to his shoulder, shouting, "Freeze, don't move!"

Punch's sudden appearance startled Bart, causing him to slosh hot coffee down the front of his long johns. Ted was also startled, but after dropping his cup, he went for his gun and fired a hurried shot. Ted's bullet whizzed by Punch's head just as Punch fired his Winchester and a split second later Ted was bowled over backwards when the .44 caliber slug slammed into his chest. Bart ran toward the gun belt by his saddle as Punch automatically racked another round into his Winchester and fired a second round. Bart let out an agonizing scream and collapsed in the dirt as the bullet drilled through his right leg, splintering the bone. Punch worked the lever on his Winchester again and held his aim as he yelled, "Don't move or the next one will bust your head wide open!"

"I can't move! You son of a bitch!" Bart screamed as he grabbed his leg and rolled onto his back.

Punch kept his Winchester cocked and ready as he made his way through the sage and into the ravine. He stopped next to Ted's body which was sprawled on the ground, with lifeless eyes open, staring skyward, blood bubbling from the gaping hole in the left lung. Punch pried the pistol from Ted's hand and tossed it into the brush. Then he continued toward Bart.

"Is he dead? Did you kill my brother?" Bart asked; his face and voice distorted by pain.

"Is that who he was?" Punch asked.

"Yeah, he's my kid brother," Bart replied clenching his teeth.

"What was his name?"

"What's it to you?"

"When I kill a man, I like to know his name."

"It was Ted...Ted Bond...or Theodore, actually."

"Where are the other two men that were with you? The man with the patch over his eye and the half breed...where are they?"

"I don't know what you're talking about."

"Wrong answer," Punch said as he placed his boot on Bart's injured leg and pressed down.

"Alright! Alright!" Bart screamed out in pain.

"They rode on up ahead."

"To Red Bluff?"

"Yeah, they went to scout out the town and make sure we weren't riding into an ambush."

"Both of them?"

"Yeah, both of them."

"What about that extra saddle over there? Who does that belong to?" Punch asked pointing at the saddle.

"It's just an extra saddle we picked up somewhere."

"When are they gonna be back?"

"I don't know."

"Wrong answer," Punch said as he started to put his boot on Bart's leg.

"Look mister, Captain Henderson will kill me if he finds out I talked."

"You're already dead or you soon will be," Punch replied without a trace of emotions.

"You gonna kill me?

"I mean to hang you," Punch replied.

"Hang me! For what? Stealing a few horses?"

"Well, for that and for murder, and rape, women burning, and for leaving that baby back there to die! I guess you can take your pick!" Punch said in an angry voice.

"What about a trial? Hell mister, you lynch me without a trial and you ain't any better than me!" Bart smirked, but with fear in his eyes.

"Where is that grey stallion you took from the Ortez place?"

Punch asked ignoring Bart's comment.

"The captain took him."

"You took another horse from there, too. Which one was that?"

"The sorrel mare on the end there. The one with the white blaze and white socks."

"Well, I guess that's the one you'll ride to meet your maker," Punch said.

Punch walked to Bart's saddle and after tossing the six-gun into the brush, he picked up the saddle and carried it to the horses. Punch saddled the sorrel mare and left Alvin's pistol and the Winchester by the picket line in order to free his hands. Then he led the mare back to Bart, stopping along the way by the extra saddle to get the lariat that was looped over the saddle horn.

"Can you stand?"

"Hell, no!"

"Alright, I'll help you up," Punch said after placing the looped end of the lariat around Bart's neck.

Bart grimaced in pain, nearly fainted, and then cursed at Punch as he helped him to his feet and boosted him up onto the saddle.

"Now don't try riding off or I'll jerk you right out of that saddle," Punch warned.

"What about my brother? You ain't gonna just leave him there are you?" Bart asked as he glanced over at his brother's body.

"I'll see that he gets buried and I'll do the same for you, which is more than you ever did for the folks you murdered," Punch replied as he started leading the mare toward the road.

Earlier that morning, Punch spotted a large cottonwood about fifty yards further up the road from the draw where the men had camped. Punch led the sorrel mare to the tree and held its reins as he tossed the free end of the lariat over a large, sagging limb.

"Any last words?" Punch asked after taking up the slack in the rope and tying it around the trunk of the tree.

"Go to hell!" Bart replied without looking at Punch.

"I'll see you there," Punch said as he swatted the sorrel on the rump sending it off at a gallop.

Bart's face turned beet red as the rope tightened around his neck and the cottonwood limb groaned under his weight. His hands clawed at the rope and his good leg kicked violently while the other dangled like the leg on a rag doll. Punch removed his hat and his sad eyes remained glued to Bart until he quit flailing and his whole body went limp.

"Guess I should have tied his hands," Punch said to himself as he pulled out his watch to note the time of Bart's passing.

It took Punch a few minutes to settle the sorrel mare down and catch her. When he did, he led her back to the tree where Bart's body was swaying gently in the morning breeze. After cutting Bart's body down, Punch lifted it up across the saddle and led the mare back to the campsite where he laid Bart's body next to his brother's and covered them with their bedrolls. He noticed that the buzzards circling over the river had grown in numbers and he continued to watch them for a moment, wondering about their purpose. Then he mounted the sorrel mare and rode her back to where he had left Alvin.

Alvin sat up as he heard the approaching hoof beats and a look of relief appeared on his face.

"It's done," Punch said as he dismounted and let the sorrel mare wander over to get acquainted with the other horses. "But I only got two of them. According the one named, Bart, the man with the patch and the half breed rode on to Red Bluff last night."

"My mind ain't too clear, Punch. So, I'll leave our next move up to you," Alvin replied.

"You think you can ride?"

"We might have to take it a little slow, but yeah, I think so."

"Well, I reckon we best head for Red Bluff then. Hopefully there's a doctor there that can take a look at your hand and if we're lucky, we'll come across that captain and the half breed on their way back to join the other two and pick up the horses. If not, I reckon we'll find 'em in Red Bluff."

"That sounds good to me."

"But first, I best take a look at that hand again."

"It still hurts a lot, but I can move my fingers again," Alvin said managing a weak smile.

"Well, that's a good sign. I'll get my needle and thread and stitch up that open wound," Punch said smiling back. "I didn't bury that sergeant fellow or the other one. Turns out the other man is his kid brother, Theodore. Anyway, I figured rather than wasting time to burry 'em we'd wrap the bodies in their bedrolls and take 'em with us slung over a couple of those stolen horses."

After Punch washed out Alvin's wound and stitched it up, they got on their horses and rode back to the campsite.

"I reckon I'll load the bodies on two of the stoutest horses and set the others free," Punch said as he dismounted next to the two bodies and handed Alvin the reins to his horse. "Be easier than trying to string 'em along with us. We got no idea who they belong to anyway and there's plenty of water and grass along the river to hold 'em until someone comes along and takes 'em,"

"I'll give you a hand," Alvin replied.

"Probably be best if I do it alone," Punch replied. "I'd hate to have you rip open those stitches."

"Well if nothing else, I can give you a hand with the horses and hold 'em steady while you load the bodies."

"Alright," Punch agreed as he started Bart's body in the outer canvas skin of his bedroll.

Once the two bodies were loaded and securely lashed on horses, Punch walked to the river to wash his hands. The stench of death filled his nose as he made his way through the willows that hugged the river bank and when he reached the water's edge, Punch immediately spotted the flock of buzzards ripping at the body on the sand bar.

Punch waded across the shallow river shouting and waving his pistol at the buzzards. But they were reluctant to take to wing, until he was within a few feet of the sand bar.

"Lord...what a mess," Punch said to himself as he looked at the body.

Punch dipped his bandana in the water and held it over his nose as he rolled the mutilated corpse over to get a look at the face. "Must be Billy Wolf," he said aloud as he spotted the belt buckle with the initials BW on it.

Punch walked back across the river and returned a few minutes later leading a buckskin horse with the extra saddle on its back and the bedroll still tied behind the cantle. As he crossed the river, he fired a shot into the air to scare off the persistent buzzards that had already returned to their purpose. Once the body was wrapped and securely tied over the saddle, Punch crossed the river again and shortly thereafter, he and Alvin were on their way to Red Bluff with three horses in tow.

After about an hour on the road, they spotted a squatty cedar log cabin with a sod roof a short distance from the road. As they got closer a dog began warning its owners that strangers were approaching and two children that had been playing on the front porch suddenly disappeared inside along with the dog.

"Let's pay these folks a visit," Punch said. "Be nice to get rid of these bodies. Maybe we can talk these folks into burying 'em for us."

"I still ain't thinking too clearly, Punch. So, I'll let you do the talking," Alvin said as he remained slumped forward in the saddle.

"Hello!" Punch yelled loudly when he and Alvin stopped their horses in front of the cabin.

Although they saw no one, Punch and Alvin were certain that behind the shuttered windows someone was peering at them through the gun slots with guns ready.

"Hold up your badge so they can see it, Alvin," Punch said. Then punch shouted, "Texas Rangers! We just want to talk to you!"

"What do you want?" came a young voice from inside the cabin.

"Just want to talk," Punch repeated.

The door to the cabin opened slightly and the barrel of a shotgun appeared first followed by a freckle faced boy, dressed in faded coveralls, with a shock of red hair protruding from his worn out cap.

"Come on out, Son, we ain't gonna harm you. This is Ranger Witherspoon and I'm Punch Masters."

"Are those dead bodies you got slung over those horses?" the boy asked in a nervous voice.

"Yeah, I'm afraid so."

"Y'all the ones that killed 'em?"

"More or less," Punch replied. "Are your folks around?"

"No Sir, Misses Johnson, our neighbors up the road a bit...she's havin' a baby. So, my pa took my Maw over there to have her help deliver it. They left me here to look after my two sisters."

"When do you reckon your pa will be back?"

"I don't know," the boy said shrugging his shoulders.

"Well, we were hoping maybe we could leave these bodies here for your pa to bury. One of 'em is getting pretty rank. We'd let you keep the horses and saddles for your trouble. You suppose your pa would be up for that? "

"Heck yeah, for three horses and saddles!"

"Alright, we'll leave 'em with you then. But, you gotta give me your word that you'll give 'em a proper burying."

"Yes Sir, I promise to burry 'em proper," the freckle faced boy said eagerly. "I could get started digging the graves right away."

"Okay, get me some paper and something to write with so I can write you out a note to prove the horses are yours and then Ranger Witherspoon will sign it to make it all legal."

Punch and Alvin dismounted as the boy went back inside the cabin and when he returned with a piece of paper and pencil, his two sisters, and the dog followed him outside.

"Are you a real Texas Ranger?" the older of the two girls asked staring at Alvin.

"Yep," Alvin replied pointing at his badge

"What's wrong with your hand?"

"Don't ask so many questions, Becky. Can't you see he ain't feeling good?"

"I got snake bit," Alvin replied trying to smile at the girl.

"Son, you think you could get some clean water and soap for Ranger Witherspoon so's he could clean up that hand and put a clean dressing on it," Punch asked as he took the paper and pencil.

"Yes, Sir, and the stove is still hot if you want me to heat up the water," the boy replied.

"I'd appreciate that, Son,"

"I can get it," Becky said with an enthusiastic look.

"Okay, but be careful and don't burn yourself," the boy warned. "Heat up the water in that copper kettle and pour it in that pan Maw uses to wash dishes in."

"I know how to do it!" Becky said giving her brother an irritated look.

"What's your pa's name Son, I want to write it on this note," Punch asked as Becky hurried back into the cabin with her younger sister trailing close behind her.

"Orville Haynes, Sir. Same as mine," the boy replied.

"I reckon that makes you Orville Junior, then," Punch said chuckling as he stopped writing and looked up from the paper.

"Yes, Sir, but everyone just calls me Junior."

"Well Junior, I imagine your pa will be pretty happy to get those three horses."

"Yes, Sir, I still get the saddles too, don't I?"

"Yep, that was part of the deal," Punch chuckled again.

Once Punch finished writing the note, he handed it to Alvin. Alvin signed it and handed it to the boy saying, "Here you are, Son. Make sure you keep it in a safe place."

"Yes Sir."

The boy folded the note and carried it inside and returned carrying the pan of water with Becky following close behind him carrying a bar of lye soap and a couple of thin dish towels with frayed edges.

While Becky and Alvin went to work cleaning his hand, Punch and Junior led the horses a short distance from the cabin and once the bodies were laid out side by side on the ground, Punch and the boy took the horses back to a makeshift corral which was beside a poorly constructed barn and unsaddled them.

"Well I guess that about does it, Son. So, I reckon we'll be on our way now. I appreciate you helping us out," Punch said shaking the boy's hand.

"Hey mister... who were those men?"

"They were a bad bunch, Son. Murderers, horse thieves, and violators of women," Punch replied. "Their names were Bartholomew Bond, Theodore Bond, and Billy Wolf. You think you can remember their names or do you want me to write 'em out for you?"

"No sir, I can remember."

"Good... I'm not sure I can spell Bartholomew, anyway,"

Punch said with a short chuckle.

Punch and Alvin were glad to be rid of their extra responsibilities and once they were back on the road they hastened the pace of their horses. It was still early in the afternoon when they arrived at the outskirts of Red Bluff. Alvin removed his badge and tucked it into shirt pocket in order to avoid drawing attention to themselves as they rode into town. They stopped a man walking along the boardwalk and asked if there was a doctor in town. The man nodded and after giving Punch and Alvin directions to the doctor's house, they rode directly to it. The doctor had Punch sit in the front room while he led Alvin into a side room to examine his hand. About an hour passed before the doctor walked back into the room.

"What do you think, Doc?" Punch asked as the doctor removed a blood stained white apron, and started rolling down the sleeves on his white shirt.

"I can see you're no surgeon and you're not much of a seamstress either, Mister Masters," the Doctor said peering over his spectacles at Punch. "But, you probably did the right thing by amputating that finger."

Punch smiled and let out a sigh of relief when he heard the doctor's comment. Then he asked, "He's gonna be okay though ain't he, Doc?"

"Yes, he should be fine as long as that wound doesn't get infected. I cleaned it out with some antiseptic and gave him a shot to help fight off the possibility of infection."

"How long before he's back to normal, Doc."

"Well, I had to put him under in order to trim back the bone a little better and stitch his hand up the proper way. So, he'll likely sleep for another hour before the chloroform starts to wear off. And he'll probably be pretty nauseous for a while after that. But by morning, he should start to feel better and I'll give him something for the pain."

"Thanks Doc, what do I owe you for taking care of him?"

"I found this Ranger Star in Mister Witherspoon's shirt pocket," the doctor said looking Punch in the eyes as he pulled Alvin's badge from his vest pocket. "Is he really a Texas Ranger?"

"Yes Sir."

"Well, I reckon there won't be any charge for my services, then. However, I would like to be reimbursed for the medical supplies I used. But, we can take care of that in the morning."

"Okay, thanks Doc."

"Suppose there was a reason, Mister Witherspoon wasn't wearing his badge, so I won't mention he's a Ranger to anyone. But, mind if I ask what brings you to Red Bluff?"

"We're lookin' for a man with a big scar on his face and a patch over his left eye."

"I know practically everyone in town and there's nobody like that living here in Red Bluff."

"Well, I don't think he's from here, Doc. I 'm pretty sure he and the rest of his gang were just passin' through. Probably on their way to the New Mexico Territory."

"I see. What's he done?"

"Murder, rape, horse thievery, and probably a lot more we ain't even aware of," Punch replied.

"Sounds like a real bad hombre."

"Yes Sir, the worst I ever heard of."

"I'll keep my eyes peeled for him," the doctor said. "I guess you'll be around town for a few days won't you?"

"Yes Sir, I aim to find that man."

"Have you found a place to stay yet?"

"Not yet. We came straight over here when we got to town."

"Well there's the Red Bluff Hotel and Saloon on Main Street, but if you want something a little quieter, Misses Malory runs a boarding house over on River Street and she's a mighty fine cook, too. She usually has rooms available because she's real particular about who she rents to. But, you tell her I sent you...and I'm sure she'll rent you a room."

"Thanks Doc. What about a livery stable?"

"Other end of town...right on Main Street."

"Thanks again Doc. I'll see you in the morning."

As Punch rode through town leading Alvin's horse, he looked at the horses tied in front of the various businesses along Main Street, hoping to spot the grey stallion and when he got to the livery stable, he did the same. But, the grey was nowhere to be seen. After stripping the saddlebags from both horses, Punch pulled his and Alvin's Winchesters from the saddle scabbards. Then he left the horses in the care of the stable hand and walked to the Misses Malory's boarding house.

"I don't allow no chewing, no smoking, no women, no cussing, no boots on the bed, and take off those spurs," Misses Malory said in a firm voice as she showed Punch the room.

"Yes Ma'am," Punch replied somewhat amused, but trying not to show it.

"Supper's at six o'clock sharp, so don't be late."

"No, Ma'am," Punch replied with a straight face. "But actually, I'll probably skip supper tonight. I got some business in town I need to tend to."

"Suit yourself. Supper is included in the price of the room whether you eat it or not is up to you."

"I understand," Punch replied.

After leaving the saddlebags and rifles in his room, Punch walked back to Main Street and sat on the bench in front of the Citizens Bank to keep an eye out for the grey and or a man with a patch over his eye. After about an hour with no sign of the grey or the captain, he walked to Red Bluff Hotel & Saloon. He paused at the swinging doors and gazed around the smoke filled saloon until he noticed the bartender staring at him with a suspicious look on his face as he wiped off glasses and stacked them on the end of the bar.

"What'll you have, mister?" the bartender asked when Punch walked up to the bar.

"Whiskey," Punch replied as he again looked around the room.

"Got two kinds," the bartender said. "One good enough and one better. The good stuff is two bits and the better stuff is a nickel more."

"I'll take the better stuff," Punch replied, turning his attention back to the bartender.

"You looking for somebody?" the bartender asked after filling a shot glass and setting it on the bar.

"Yeah, a man with a big scar on his face and a patch over his left eye," Punch said after downing the whiskey and motioning for a second.

"You a friend of his?" the bartender asked as he refilled the glass.

"Not particularly," Punch said, looking the bartender in the eyes.

After a momentary uncomfortable silence, Punch reached into his pocket and pulled out a five dollar gold piece.

"How about it? You seen a man with a patch over his eye?" Punch asked as he slapped the coin on the bar.

The bartender looked down the bar in both directions and then he covered the coin with the towel he was using to wipe off the glasses. After sweeping the coin into his hand, he leaned closer to Punch; his breath reeked of tobacco and cheap whiskey.

"He came in here late last night, had a couple of drinks, and asked if I knew anybody that might be interested in buying some horses," the bartender said in a voice just above a whisper.

"So, what about it? Do know anybody that might be interested in his horses?"

"Yeah, I told him about a man named Max Horner. Max is always in the market for horses."

"How do I find Max Horner's place?"

"Well it ain't hard to find, but I reckon if you was to just hang around here a bit, that man with the patch will be back. He's still got a room upstairs."

"Okay, how much for a bottle?"

"I'll give you this one for a dollar. It's nearly half full."

Punch flipped the bartender a dollar. Then he carried his glass and the bottle to a table where he could sit with his back to the wall and watch the door. Punch had barely sat down when one of gals that worked in the saloon hustling drinks and selling companionship approached the table. She was a rather attractive woman, probably in her mid- twenties, with bottle blond hair, and two coats of paint on her face.

"How about some company, cowboy?" she asked leaning over to show that she was well endowed.

Punch smiled as he removed his hat and said politely, "No

thanks, Ma'am. I ain't really lonely and besides that, my wife told me not to talk to any pretty women while I was away from home."

"You always do what your wife tells you?" the woman asked chuckling.

"Yes, Ma'am!" Punch replied still smiling.

"Well, if you change your mind...my name is Ginger." She said laughing softly before moving on to find a more lucrative customer.

Punch was not the type of man that needed to find courage in a bottle. He drank whiskey because he enjoyed it, but he was very aware of its effect on him and he knew his limit. So as he watched the door, Punch sipped his whiskey at a rate that barely kept his lips moist. He knew there was killing to be done and the trick was making sure he wasn't the one killed. Although Punch had killed more than his share of men during the war and few more after it ended, he had never stood face to face in a showdown where the speed of a man's draw determined the outcome. In reality, Punch was plenty fast and faster than most. On his sixth birthday his father had presented Punch and his twin brother, Homer, with pistols that he had painstakingly whittled out of wood along with holster rigs made from leather strapping and a burlap feed sack. Punch and his brother spent countless hours drawing against each other and as a result, by the time they went off to join the confederacy, they were both a couple of accomplished pistoleros. But they quickly learned that being able to hit what you aimed at, was much more important than the speed at which you could get a pistol to clear leather.

Punch was just about to refill his glass when a man with a patch over his left eye parted the swinging doors and stepped into the saloon. Punch sat up straight studying the man. The expression on the man's face was one of contempt and arrogance, but Punch was too far away to tell if there was a scar on the man's face. As the man continued toward the bar, he carried himself in a confident manner and his walk had a certain swagger to it, like what you would expect from a military officer. Although, Punch had never laid eyes on Captain Warren Henderson before, he was certain that the man walking toward the bar was in fact the notorious killer he was after.

When the bartender saw the man walking toward the bar, he glanced at Punch and gave him a quick nod as if he was trying to send a signal and then quickly turned his attention back to the man as he reached the bar. Punch slid his right hand off the table to ensure the hammer strap on his holster was off. Then he gripped the pistol and eased it up slightly just enough to ensure it was free. Punch continued to watch Henderson as he spoke to the bartender, but Punch could not hear their words. The bartender filled a shot glass with the good stuff. Henderson gulped it down and motioned for another. Ginger suddenly appeared out of a dark corner and laid her hand on the Henderson's shoulder as she walked up behind him with a flirtatious smile. She said something, probably something suggestive to the captain as she moved to his side, but her expression quickly changed as she saw Henderson's disfigured face, the scar, and the patch over his eye. Punch saw her expression change and so did Henderson. The captain's face grew angry and he grabbed Ginger by the arm, cursing at her in a furious voice. Then he jerked her closer to him and pressed his scared face against hers as he let out an evil laugh and began kissing her neck while groped her breasts with his free hand. Ginger screamed and tried to pull free, but she could not break his grip. Punch got to his feet, as did a young cowboy seated at a table near the bar just few feet from the captain.

"Let her go!" the young cowboy shouted.

The captain shoved Ginger aside and turned to face the cowboy. Then with lightening like speed, he pulled the Schofield revolver from the holster on his hip, cocked it, and had it pointed at the young cowboy's head before the cowboy could even blink. The young cowboy raised his hands and slowly started backing away with fear in his eyes. The other men at the table quickly stood and moved away from the cowboy to avoid being hit by a stray bullet. Henderson suddenly turned and pointed his revolver at the bartender when he noticed the bartender reaching under counter. The bartender quickly raised his hands and retreated away from the bar with a panicked expression.

"Best mind your own business barkeep, unless you want to die, too!" the captain scowled with a threatening look.

Punch was half way to the bar with his pistol ready to fire when Henderson again turned his attention to the cowboy.

"Hold it right there Henderson!" Punch shouted as the captain raised his pistol and took aim at the cowboy's face with every intention of killing him.

Henderson froze in his tracks and slowly looked over his shoulder. Then he holstered his Schofield before turning to face Punch.

"Do you know me?" Henderson asked glaring at Punch with an angry look.

"I know of you," Punch replied. "You're a horse thief, murderer, rapist, woman burner, and baby killer. And I guess that's all I need to know."

"You some kind of lawman?"

"Nope, just a Texan who aims to see you pay for the things you've done."

"Well Tex, looks like you have me at a disadvantage!" the captain smirked. "So what do you intend to do now?"

Punch was silent for a moment as he thought about his options. He wanted in the worst way to merely pull the trigger, but he couldn't bring himself to just shoot the captain.

"I guess we got two choices," Punch said as he lowered the hammer on his Colt and slowly holstered it. "I can take you back to Pecos to stand trial and hang or..."

The young cowboy quickly moved from behind the captain and the saloon grew silent. Henderson smiled an evil taunting smile and laughed a wicked laugh as he glared at Punch with his one good eye, then without so much as a twitch, he went for his gun. Punch had his gun up, cocked, and he was just about to pull the trigger when he heard the Schofield roar and felt a searing pain as the captain's bullet grazed his left arm. Punch fired and the captain stumbled backward. Punch fired again, and again, and again until the hammer fell on a spent cartridge. The smell of burnt powder filled the saloon and gun smoke burned Punch's eyes as he gazed across the saloon. Henderson's body was sprawled across the table previously occupied by the young cowboy and his friends.

Punch ejected the spent cartridges from his Colt and then replaced them one at time as he walked the remaining distance across the saloon. When he reached the table where the captain's body lay in a growing puddle of blood and saw the six gaping holes in his chest, he holstered his pistol, up righted the chair next to the table, and let out a long sigh as he sat down.

Chapter Four

The sky was a dull gray with low hanging clouds. Rain had fallen earlier, but now only an occasional drizzle or mist fell from the clouds. Duv and most of the hired hands were sitting on the porch of the bunkhouse, smoking, talking, and enjoying an unexpected day off.

"Rider coming," one of the men said as he was refilling his pipe and just happened to glance down the road toward Pecos.

"Probably another drifter looking for work," Duv said after running his tongue along the paper of the cigarette he had just finished rolling.

The men continued talking, occasionally glancing back up the road to check the progress of the approaching rider. When the rider reached the entrance to the Double M Ranch and turned his chestnut colored Morgan off of the main road, Duv left the porch of the bunkhouse and walked to the front of the main ranch house to find out what the rider wanted.

"Howdy, what can I do for you?" Duv asked loudly.

When the rider raised his head and his face was no longer hidden by the large brim on his Stetson, Duv immediately recognized the man even before he spoke.

"How are you, Duv?"

"Well, I'll be damned! Alvin Witherspoon, how the hell are you?"

"A little wet at the moment, but otherwise I'm doin' fine," Alvin replied as he dismounted.

"You still a Texas Ranger?"

"Yep, I'm a sergeant now," Alvin said pulling back his slicker to reveal his Ranger Badge. "But to be honest, I been thinking of calling it quits. Seems like, anymore the criminals got more rights than law abiding citizens."

"Have you heard about, Punch?" Duv asked as he and Alvin firmly shook hands.

"Yeah, I was in Pecos dropping off a prisoner. Marshal Scott told me about it. I sure was shocked. Wish, I would have found out in time to be here when he was laid to rest."

"Well, there was a good turnout for his funeral. Must have been nearly fifty folks here," Duv said with sadness showing in his eyes.

"How'd it happen, exactly?"

"Well, I'm not sure if you know about all the rain and flash flooding we had back in the early spring."

"Not really. Until this week, I been spending most of my time up around Abilene and it's been pretty dry up that way."

"Seems like it rained for nearly a week straight down here. It rained so much that most of the dry gullies and arroyos were full of water and the river was out of its banks. Anyway, about half of the cows that were bred last summer had already calved and the others were due to calf at any time. We were afraid some of the young calves might get swept away if they were down in the gullies and got caught in a down pour, so we moved all the cows with calves and the ones that were pregnant to a forty acre parcel we fenced in last fall that's up on that hill yonder. Anyway, the night before it happened we had another terrible rainstorm. Punch wanted me and the boys to concentrate on getting the roof repaired on the barn. So, Punch, rode out alone to check on the cows and see if any more of 'em had calved during the night. Me and the boys took a break when it got to be a little past noon and that's when it dawned on us that Punch hadn't come back. I just kinda figured he probably come across a cow that was havin' trouble giving birth and maybe he was tied up pulling a calf. Wouldn't be the first time Punch or one of us had to pull a calf. So, none of us was really concerned, but I decided to ride out and see if he needed a hand. Well, when I got out there, I spotted his horse, but I didn't see hide nor hair of Punch."

Duv paused and fished a bandana out of his pocket to catch a sniffle and then in a crackling voice he said, "I found him about a half hour later, lying face down in the mud...He'd been shot in the back."

"Any idea who might have been responsible?"

"Not a clue," Duv said shaking his head. "You know Punch... he spoke his mind which riled a few folks now and then, but he never crossed anybody on purpose. And anytime someone needed help... Punch was the first one to pitch in. So as far as I know, he didn't have any real enemies."

"Did you see any tracks or sign of any kind?"

"Yeah, after I brought Punch's body back here, me and a couple of the boys rode back out there to see if we could find any sign and we found a fresh set of tracks from the road up to the top of the hill and I found a spent 44-40 shell, too. Me and the men followed those tracks and they led us all the way to Pecos. But once we got close to town, there were so many other tracks and the road was so muddy that they just blended in with the others. So about all we could do was to let Marshal Scott know about Punch's murder and then we rode back here to the ranch. And so far, I'm afraid Punch's murder is pretty much a dead end."

"Yeah, that's what Marshal Scott told me, too," Alvin said shaking his head in disbelief. "Hell of a way for a man like Punch to die."

"Yep, sure was," Duv said nodding with his head held low.

"How's Willow?" Alvin asked.

"About the way you would expect, I reckon. She's a strong woman, but she took losing Punch awful hard. Never saw a woman that loved a man any more than she loved Punch."

"They were a match made in heaven, alright. That's for sure," Alvin said with a sad look. "How about Luke?"

"He tried to take it like a man. But, he sure loved his pa and I know he shed a lot of tears when he was off alone," Duv said. "Hell, I guess we all did. I'm kinda surprised you didn't cross paths with Luke on your way here. He and his misses took the wagon to Pecos to visit her pa and get a load of lumber."

"Misses?! When did that happen?"

"About a month after Punch died. She's the daughter of a preacher over in Pecos. We plan on starting to build a house for 'em tomorrow. Providing the weather cooperates. Anyway, I imagine they'll be back soon."

"Well, I'll be damned," Alvin chuckled.

"How about you, Alvin? You married yet?" Duv asked.

"No, an old friend once told me, wives are like the flowers on a prickly pear cactus. They're pretty to look at, but you're better off not picking one."

"Well, I got no complaints," Duv said after a short laugh. "Don't guess you know I got two little boys now."

"Good for you, Duv. I guess a lot has changed since the last time I was here," Alvin said smiling.

"Been about ten years, ain't it?" Duv replied.

"Has it really been ten years?"

"Sure has. Last time I saw you was when you and Punch went after those four men that stole a bunch of horses and killed all those folks."

"I ain't forgot. Hell, that's when I lost my finger. I just didn't realize it had been ten years. My god...where has the time gone?" Alvin said shaking his head. "Well, I guess I best go pay my respects to, Willow,"

"Go ahead. I'm sure she'll be glad to see you," Duv said. "You plan on staying the night?"

"Yeah, probably so."

"Alright, I'll unsaddle your horse and put him in the barn."

"Thanks, Duv."

Alvin walked up to the house and used the boot scraper by the steps before continuing up onto the porch. After removing his hat and slicking back his wet hair he knocked loudly on the door. He was just about to knock again when the door opened.

"Hello...can I help you?" the young lady that answered the door asked.

Alvin's eyes grew wide with surprise as he looked at the young lady. Then with a big smile he asked, "Lucy... is that really you?"

"Yes... and who might you be?"

"I can't believe my eyes. You're all grown up," Alvin said shaking his head in amazement.

"Do I know you?" Lucy asked with a puzzled look.

"Forgive me...I'm Alvin Witherspoon. I was a friend of your..."

"Ranger Alvin Witherspoon?" Lucy interrupted with a big smile.

"That's right," Alvin said opening his slicker to reveal the badge pinned on his shirt. "I can't get over the fact that you're a young lady now. The last time I saw you...you were just a skinny little girl in pigtails."

"I was only nine or ten back then. I'm almost twenty one now," Lucy said after a short laugh.

"Who was at the door, Lucy?" Willow asked as she walked into the parlor from the kitchen.

A large smile crossed Alvin's face as he saw Willow. Willow stopped a moment with a shocked look on her face and then she rushed across the room with open arms.

"Best let me pull off this slicker before you go to hugging me," Alvin warned quickly.

"Lucy, help Alvin take his coat off," Willow said beaming with happiness as she stepped back and looked Alvin over from head to toe.

"My boots are kinda muddy, too. I hate to track up your whole house," Alvin said blushing.

"Don't worry about the floor. It can always be mopped," Willow said as Lucy hung Alvin's slicker on the hall tree.

Alvin stood there with his arms pinned to his side while Willow hugged him and after kissing him on the cheek, she grabbed his hand and pulled him through the doorway.

"You look like you finally gained a little weight," Willow said as she again looked Alvin over without his coat.

"I don't spend quite as much time on the trail as I used too and I guess age has something to do with that, too," Alvin laughed.

"Gosh how long has it been?"

"It's been over ten years, Mama. We were just talking about that," Lucy replied before Alvin could speak.

"Yes, I guess it has." Willow replied still smiling. "What do you think of my little girl, Alvin, now that she's all grown up?"

"She's practically the spittin' image of you, Willow."

"Well, not quite anymore. No need to pretend you haven't noticed the strands of gray in my hair. But, she does look a lot like I did when I was her age," Willow said gazing at Lucy and smiling.

"Well, the years have been kind to you, Willow. You're still a mighty handsome woman." Alvin said smiling with a hint of redness in his face. Then glancing at Lucy he added, "Matter of fact, you're both mighty handsome."

"You're too kind, Alvin," Willow said gently touching Alvin's cheek with the back of her hand. "You'll have supper with us and stay the night won't you?"

"If it's no trouble. I ugh... I really just wanted to come by to pay my respects and offer my condolences. But... it would be nice to visit awhile."

"It's no trouble. You know you're always welcome," Willow said smiling.

"I wish, I would have heard about ...Well, I'm just sorry I wasn't here for the funeral, Willow."

"I know, Alvin. I guess that's my fault. I should have sent a telegram to Ranger Headquarters or tried to get word to you somehow. I guess I just didn't have all my wits about me."

"Well, by the time the telegram caught up to me and I was able to get here...I probably would have missed the funeral anyhow," Alvin said with an understanding smile. "Anyway, I sure am sorry about your loss... Punch, was a hell of a man!"

"Thank you, Alvin. Punch thought a lot of you, too," Willow said as tears started to build in her eyes. Then in a much happier voice she said, "Lucy, why don't you show Alvin to the spare bedroom and then we best figure out what we'll have for supper."

"Okay, Mama."

"If you don't mind... I'd like to walk down and see Punch's grave first," Alvin said.

"I'll go with you," Willow said. "Just let me grab an umbrella and shawl."

"I'd kinda like to go alone, if that's okay?" Alvin replied.

"Of course," Willow said after seeing the sadness in Alvin's eyes. "When you come back, just let yourself in. Lucy and I will be in the kitchen."

A light mist started to fall again as Alvin walked to the white washed fence that wrapped around what had grown to become the Double M cemetery. In the back row were the headstones of Art Wadsworth, Jack Wilson, and Douglas "Dallas" Thomas, who were the three cowboys that were killed when rustlers stole Punch's cattle a dozen or so years back. In the front row, on the right side, were the headstones of Punch's twin brother, Homer, who was Willow's first husband and next to it was the headstone of their son, Johnny who had perished in the same fire as Homer. Punch's grave was in the front row, but on the opposite end of the plot. At first Alvin thought it odd that Punch's grave was such a distance from the other headstones, but after a moment of thought, a weak smile crossed his face when he realized that the placement was exactly as Willow must have wanted it which would allow for Willow to be laid to rest next to Punch on his right, with enough space left for Lucy to be laid to rest next to her brother Johnny, and room for Luke on Punch's left.

Alvin removed his hat as he swung the gate open and walked to Punch's grave. A single bouquet of fresh blue bonnets and Indian paint brushes lay on top of the red dirt at the base of Punch's headstone.

"No doubt, Willow's doing," Alvin thought to himself.

He could feel his eyes starting to well up and then a few tears mixed with the rain drops streaming down his cheeks.

"Hell of an ending for such a brave man," Alvin said aloud as if Punch were listening. "But, I know you'd be the first to say nothing is forever, Punch, and at least you were laid to rest near your loved ones....There's a lot to be said about that," Alvin added as he thought briefly about where he might be laid to rest when his time came.

Alvin remained at the grave for several minutes until the drizzle turned to a steady down pour of rain. At which time, he placed his right hand on the tombstone, looked up at the sky, and said, "Save me a place, Punch. You never know when I might be comin' your way."

When Alvin reached the ranch house, he again used the boot scraper to clean the mud from the soles of his boots before walking up on the porch, but after noticing the muddy tracks that followed him to the door, he sat down in one of the rockers and pulled off his boots. After noticing a sizeable hole in his left sock next to his big toe, he twisted the sock until the hole was on the bottom of his foot and then removed his wet slicker and draped it over the back of the rocker before reaching for the door knob. Once inside, he removed his hat and gun belt which he hung on the hall tree. He was just about to announce his return when he remembered how he and Punch shared part of a jug several years back. He lifted the lid to the hall tree bench and big grin crossed his face as he spotted the jug of whiskey inside.

"I thought I heard someone in here," Willow said. "Were you looking for something, Alvin?"

"Not really, Willow. I was just reminiscing," Alvin said still grinning as he lowered the lid on the bench.

Luke and his wife, Mary, arrived a short time later. Luke remembered Alvin right away and the exchange that followed was what you would expect from two long lost friends.

"Mary this is Alvin Witherspoon," Luke said in a proud tone as he introduced his wife to Alvin. "As you can see he's a Texas Ranger."

Mary was a pretty young lady with blond hair and deep blue eyes, but her good looks were much different than Willow's and Lucy's. She also had a certain innocent and delicate look which made Alvin smile as he thought to himself that her appearance was exactly like what a preacher's daughter should look like.

"Nice to meet you, Mister Witherspoon. Or should I call you Ranger Witherspoon?"

"How about just plain, Alvin?"

"Okay Alvin." Mary said with a warm smile.

"Luke, why don't the three of you go into the parlor," Willow suggested. "You're just under foot here in the kitchen, anyway."

"Is there something I can do?" Mary asked.

"No thanks, Mary," Willow replied. "Lucy and I can manage. You go keep Luke and Alvin company."

Although Willow's tone was pleasant enough, Alvin sensed that Mary had not yet been fully accepted as part of the family.

"Remember that story I told you about my pa and a Ranger going after those men that were killing folks, raping women, and stealing horses?" Luke asked Mary once they were in the parlor.

"Yes, I remember. It was a dreadful story!" Mary said, her expression showing her displeasure.

"Alvin was that Ranger." Luke said in an excited voice.

"Well as it turned out, I was just along for the ride. Punch... Luke's pa deserves all the credit," Alvin said quickly. Then trying to change the subject he asked, "Mary, I understand your father is a preacher."

"Yes, he's a Baptist Minister," Mary replied smiling.

"Has he been a minister long?"

"About six years. He took up the good book and started preaching shortly after my mother died. Before that he was a bartender."

"That's quite a change," Alvin chuckled and then blushed as he thought less of his comment.

"Yes, papa always said mama's passing was his wake up call from Jesus."

"How long have you lived in Pecos?"

"They just moved to Pecos about six months ago," Luke said before Mary could reply.

"And the two of you have already been married for a month," Alvin said visibly surprised. Then smiling to hide his surprise he quickly added, "Must have been love at first sight."

"More like lust at first sight," Lucy muttered to herself in the kitchen when she overheard the conversation.

"I guess it was," Luke said taking Mary's hand and looking into her eyes.

"How about you, Alvin? How long have you been a Ranger?" Mary asked.

"A long time...about sixteen years, I reckon."

"Wow, that is a long time," Mary replied.

"Yeah, and I'm beginning to think it's been too long."

"You ain't thinking of quitting the Rangers are you, Alvin?" Luke asked with a surprised look.

"Matter of fact, I been giving it some consideration."

"What are you going to do?"

"Well, I was talking to Marshal Scott in Pecos earlier today. He's not in the best of health you know. Anyway, he told me he's thinking of quitting. So, I thought if he does...why I might throw my hat into the ring. Of course, it would be up to the mayor and town council as to whether or not I got the job."

"They'd be fools not to hire you!" Luke said with a sparkle in his eyes. "Maybe, I could be your deputy."

"Absolutely not!" Mary said quickly.

"You'd be crazy to leave what you got here, Luke!" Alvin said with a judgmental look. "Most men work their whole lives trying to scrape together enough money to buy a little land and start up ranch. And here you are with one already built up just sitting in your lap. Your pa would roll over in his grave if you walked away from this place!"

"It was just a thought...I wasn't serious," Luke said blushing slightly.

Once supper was ready, Alvin, Luke, and Mary joined Willow and Lucy at the large table in the kitchen for a delicious meal of baked ham, mashed potatoes, green beans, with freshly baked hot bread and peach cobbler for desert. The meal and lively conversation around the table made for an enjoyable evening and the time passed very quickly. It was nearly nine o'clock by the time they realized the hour and while the women cleaned up the kitchen, Luke and Alvin headed for the front porch, stopping briefly to get the jug from the hall tree.

"After you, Alvin," Luke said as he handed the jug to Alvin once they were seated in adjoining rockers.

"That's some mighty fine shine," Alvin said after taking a healthy drink. "You still get it from that same old Mexican man that used to deliver it in a donkey drawn cart?"

"No, that was Mister Sanchez. He died about two years ago. We get it from his son Pedro. It's the same recipe, but he don't deliver it in a cart no more. His business has grown so much that he needs a wagon to make his rounds."

"I'm not surprised. It's good stuff, alright," Alvin said handing the jug back to Luke.

"Yeah, pa used to say it was better than most of the whiskey that comes in the bottles with fancy labels," Luke said after taking a swig and handing the jug back to Alvin.

"You know...the last time I had a drink with your pa, it was right here on this porch. We drank out of a jug just like this and I remember Punch saying something like, 'Whiskey drinking should be done in moderation except in the company of unwanted or boring company.' Or something like that," Alvin laughed. "Anyway, I'm glad to see some of Punch's traditions are still alive."

"I doubt much will change as long as my Aunt Willow has a say in things," Luke replied after joining Alvin in laughter.

"She's a fine woman. I really admire her spirit," Alvin replied smiling.

"Yeah and Lucy is turning out to be exactly like her."

"I can't get over how she's grown," Alvin chuckled. "And the resemblance between them is amazing."

"It ain't just their looks that are the same. They even think alike. And if something is on their minds... Well, let's just say... they're both pretty outspoken."

"I imagine that makes things pretty interesting around here at times!" Alvin laughed.

"Interesting ain't the word for it. Pa had a hard enough time when it was just Aunt Willow he had to answer to. Now it's just me...and I gotta deal with both of them! And a wife to boot!"

"Well, I reckon bein' around three attractive women comes with a price," Alvin laughed.

A short time later Luke and Alvin were joined by the ladies, but the damp, cool air drove them back inside after just a few minutes on the porch. And when Luke's wife informed him she was going to bed, he joined her leaving Alvin alone on the porch with only the jug as company.

"Here's to you, Punch," Alvin said lifting the jug for one last time before replacing the cork.

Alvin sat quietly for quite some time after the others had all gone to bed, gazing up at the stars, and watching the few wisps of thin clouds streak across the mostly clear sky. He turned toward the door when he heard it open and then stood up as Lucy walked onto the porch with a blanket wrapped around her nightgown.

"I wondered if you were still out here," she said.

"Yeah, I wasn't sleepy. Truth is... I generally have trouble going to sleep on most nights. Too much on my mind, I reckon," Alvin said. "What about you? How come you ain't asleep?"

"To be honest I was, but then I woke up when Luke and Mary...Well, let's just say the walls between our rooms are real thin."

"I see," Alvin said grinning. "Well, I'd enjoy the company if you want to set awhile."

"It usually doesn't take them very long," Lucy said, taking the rocker next to Alvin.

"Mary seems like a real nice lady," Alvin said as he sat back down.

"I suppose," Lucy said in an unconvincing tone. "She lays on that part about being a preacher's daughter a little too thick sometimes."

"What does Willow think of her?"

"I think she likes her, alright. After all, she is Luke's wife. But, it's hard to tell for sure what she really thinks of Mary...She hasn't been herself since Uncle Punch died. Tonight was the closest I've seen her to normal since the funeral. I think seeing you kind of turned back the clock for her."

"I imagine it'll take some time, but I reckon she'll be back to her usual self after a while," Alvin said. "She's a mighty strong woman."

"I know she wasn't happy about Luke marrying Mary just a month after Uncle Punch's funeral."

"Yeah, I was surprised when I heard Mary and Luke have only known each other for six months or so."

"I'm pretty sure it was Mary's idea to get married. But at least she had enough sense to just have her father perform a simple ceremony instead of having a big church wedding."

"You don't think she's ..."

"Pregnant?" Lucy interjected. "No, but I don't think she was a virgin when they married. I overheard you talking in the parlor before supper. That part about love at first sight...Lust at first sight would be more like it! At least for Luke, but under that innocent look of Mary's...something tells me Luke wasn't her first. She seems pretty savvy about what to do between the sheets."

"Well, as long as they're happy...I guess that's all that counts." Alvin said trying to sound optimistic.

"I hope so. By the way, I also couldn't help overhearing what you said about the Rangers. Are you really thinking of leaving the Rangers?"

"Yeah, I been thinking on it for a while."

"You should have seen the look on mama's face when she heard it."

"I imagine she was surprised."

"Yes and also glad."

"Well, it ain't for certain yet."

"Why are you thinking of quitting?"

"Well, things are changing and I'm not sure I like the changes. Sometimes when you're a chasin' outlaws, you gotta stretch the law a bit to get the job done. In the past when you went after a man that was running from the law and you had to shoot him... nobody questioned it or thought anything about it. It was all part of the job. Nowadays, seems like you gotta fill out a report and answer a bunch of questions every time you even fire your gun. And god help you if you ever kill a man... even if the man is a known horse thief, cattle rustler...or even a murderer. When I first joined the Rangers, there were times when you caught men that you knew were guilty and you was out in the middle of west Texas or some other god forsaken part of the state; you could just go ahead and hang 'em. Nowadays, you gotta bring 'em in and let 'em stand trial regardless of what they done even if you got 'em dead to rights. And half the time when you do bring 'em in, some fancy lawyer with a bunch of legal mumbo jumbo gets the charges dropped and the crooks end up going free."

"What makes you think being the marshal of Pecos or any other town would be any different?"

"Might not be, but if I was the Marshal of Pecos, it would be a whole lot easier to swallow seeing a criminal that I nabbed right in town go free... instead of one that I had to chase clean across Texas and back. Besides... the pay is about the same and there's a lot to be said for sleeping in a bed with a roof over your head every night and taking your meals sitting at a table instead of sleepin' and eatin' on the cold ground out in the middle of the prairie somewhere. I don't know... maybe I'm just getting too old for rangerin'."

"How old are you, Alvin?"

"I just turned thirty five."

"That's not old," Lucy laughed.

"Maybe not in actual years, but some mornings I feel more like fifty five," Alvin laughed.

"Well, I guess it's been long enough by now. I sure will be glad when their house gets built and they move into it," Lucy said.

"How about you, Lucy? You got a steady bo?"

"Not really."

"I figure a young lady with your looks would have suitors lining up," Alvin chuckled.

"Well, I get asked out occasionally, but there's not much to choose from out here in the middle of nowhere," Lucy said smiling. "I don't get much chance to meet men except when we go to church or once a month when I get to go to Mentone or Pecos."

"How about you Ranger Alvin Witherspoon, you got a steady gal?"

"Nope."

"How come? Much as you get around, I would think you know lots of women."

"I reckon that's part of the problem," Alvin chuckled. "I get around too much. So, I'm never around anyplace long enough to really get to know them."

"Well, maybe that'll change if you quit the Rangers."

"It might at that."

"Well, I should be able to go back to sleep now," Lucy said smiling and placing her hand on his. Then after standing up, she added, "I'll see you in the morning, Alvin."

"Good night, Lucy," Alvin said as he also stood up. "I think I'll turn in, too."

Chapter Five

    A few days after Alvin left the Double M Ranch, the stagecoach was held up between Peyote and the town of Monahans for the third time in about the same number of months. During each of the hold ups the robbers wore masks, but based on the descriptions of the three robbers and their horses which were provided by the driver, shotgun guard, and passengers, there was no question that the robberies were committed by the same three men. After each hold up, once the stage reached Monahans with news of the hold up, the county sheriff organized a posse and went after the robbers, but the Texas state line was just a little over thirty miles away and by the time the posse backtracked to where the robbery had occurred and then proceeded to follow the bandit's tracks, the robbers were already in the New Mexico Territory. As a result, the hold ups and subsequent chases amounted to little more than a cat and mouse game between the sheriff and the robbers. No one had been hurt during the first two robberies, but during the third robbery the frustrated shotgun rider, who had also been guarding the coaches during the two previous holdups, was killed when he tried to shoot it out with the bandits. The sheriff again gave chase, but after returning to Monahans empty handed, he sent a telegram to the Texas Rangers asking for help and the following day, Alvin Witherspoon was dispatched to Monahans to take over the case. When he arrived in Monahans, Alvin spent some time with the sheriff gathering as much information about the hold ups and holdup men as the sheriff could provide. Then early the next morning, Alvin headed for the town of Kermit which was about twenty two miles away from Monahans and just five or so miles from the state line.
    Alvin was no stranger to the town of Kermit which was little more than a cluster of adobe and rough sawn, unpainted, wood structures that sprang up around the intersection of three well-traveled roads. Because of its location, Kermit was a popular stopping point for people of all sorts that were traveling to or from the New Mexico Territory. It was also a popular stopping point for bandits, horse thieves, rustlers, and other desperados fleeing from

Texas to the relative safety of the New Mexico Territory. When Alvin arrived in Kermit, he pulled his horse to a stop across the street from the charred remains of what was once the town jail and marshal's office. Alvin dismounted and tied his horse to the hitching rail in front of a plain adobe building. There was no sign of any kind on the building, but it was well known in the region as Hondo's Cantina. Alvin removed his Ranger Badge and slid it into his shirt pocket. Then he checked his pistol before proceeding to the open door of the cantina. He paused just inside of the doorway with his gun hand ready to let his eyes adjust to the dark, smoke filled room. Then he looked around the room for anyone resembling the descriptions of the stagecoach robbers. Two men seated at a table in the far corner stared at Alvin with curious eyes and then quickly looked away as they made eye contact with him. Alvin gave them each a second look before continuing to survey the dozen or more other men in the cantina. He suspected that at least half of the men in the cantina had committed crimes on at least one side of the state line, but he didn't recognize anyone in particular. As Alvin started toward the bar, the two men at the corner table stood up and made a hasty exit. Two others who were standing at the bar also left when they saw Alvin approaching.

"Ain't seen you for a while, Witherspoon," the bartender said in an agitated voice.

"You miss me, Hondo?" Alvin asked grinning.

"Not particularly," Hondo replied. "For one thing you're bad for business."

"Well, I haven't missed you either, Hondo," Alvin chuckled.

"Whiskey or tequila?" Hondo asked.

"I already know the whiskey is no good. So, I'll try the tequila."

Hondo set a glass on the bar in front of Alvin and filled it with two fingers worth of tequila. Alvin downed the liquid, made a sour face, and motioned for another as he laid a twenty dollar gold piece on the counter.

"What do you know about the three men that have been robbing the stage outside of Peyote?"

"What makes you think I know anything?" Hondo asked in a

low voice while staring at the coin on the bar.

"Don't play games with me, Hondo. I know they've been in here at least three times over the last couple of months," Alvin said after downing the second tequila. "One's short and the other two are tall. The short one is heavy set with dark hair and a beard. One of tall men has sandy hair with long sideburns. He wears a black hat with a silver concho hat band and he wears a fancy black, left handed holster rig. The other one is a husky man with dark hair and a noticeable scar on his right cheek."

"Yeah, I've seen 'em. Matter of fact they were in here three or four days ago." Hondo said as he started to pick up the twenty dollar gold piece.

"Not so fast," Alvin said grabbing Hondo's hand. "Where can I find 'em?"

"Rumor has it... they been seen around Jal quite a bit." Hondo replied as he looked around to ensure no one else was within hearing range.

"Jal?" Alvin repeated.

"Yeah, that's what I heard. Too bad it's is in New Mexico. Ain't that right, Witherspoon?" Hondo laughed.

"Yeah... too bad," Alvin said frowning as he released Hondo's hand. "Maybe, I'll just hang around here in Kermit and wait for 'em. I'm sure they'll be back... eventually."

"I doubt it. You ain't much of a stranger around these parts, Witherspoon." Hondo sneered. "Won't take long for everyone this side of the Pecos to know you're here."

Alvin knew Hondo was right, so he left the cantina, and once he was mounted, he turned his horse back toward the way he had come, but when he reached the intersection of the three roads, he stopped his horse and gazed north toward the New Mexico Territory. He knew he should head back to Monahans, but the thought of letting the fugitives go just because they were across the state line made him angry.

"The hell with it!" Alvin said aloud as he started his horse toward New Mexico.

Alvin had never been to Jal, but he remembered seeing it on a map and although he didn't know how far across the state line it was, he remembered it wasn't far. It took Alvin less than two hours to reach Jal, which to his surprise, didn't look much different than Kermit. Alvin rode slowly from one end of town to the other looking for three horses that matched the description given to the sheriff following the robberies, but he found none that were close enough to warrant a second look. So after reaching the end of town, he turned his horse around and rode back to a small cafe where the aroma of slow cooking pork, sizzling onions, and peppers caught his attention during his initial pass through town. After eating his fill of fajitas and black beans, Alvin walked across the street to the cantina to wash down his meal and to see if by chance, the stage robbers might also be there quenching their thirst. He paused briefly in the doorway to check out the six other men in the cantina. Then he walked to the bar and ordered a tequila.

"You are a stranger here, no?" the bartender asked as he filled a brown porcelain shot glass.

"Yeah, that's right. Where can a man find some action in this town?"

"What kind of action are you looking for, Señor?"

"I don't know... I was just wondering if there was more to do here in Jal on a Friday night besides drinkin' Tequila."

"That depends on how much money you have to spend, Señor."

"Well, I got a little."

"Only a little, Señor?" the bartender asked grinning. "For two dollars you can make love to a beautiful señorita. But maybe is better you wait until later and bet the two dollars on the roosters. If you are lucky maybe you could turn the two dollars into mucho más and have many señoritas."

"Roosters...you talking about cock fights?"

"Si Señor."

"What time do the cock fights start?"

"Sometime around seven o'clock, men who want to fight their roosters will come in here to show everyone the roosters. Then they will go outside and once everyone has placed their bets on the rooster they think will win, the fighting will start."

"Will there be plenty of men here to bet against?"

"Si, almost every man in town will be here and many of the

women, also."

"Okay, I reckon I'll come back later then," Alvin said after downing his tequila.

Alvin paid for his drink and rode back up the street to the livery stable where he made arrangements for his horse's keep. Then he walked to a small two story clapboard structure at the end of town which was the town's only hotel. After checking in, Alvin went up to his room where he sat by the open window watching the street and hoping to spot the three men he was after. Once the sun set and dark shadows started to consume the street, Alvin hurried down the stairs on the back side of the hotel and walked to the cantina. A group of a dozen or so women were huddled in the street outside the cantina talking, mostly in Spanish, and laughing. Alvin tipped his hat as he walked by, but most of the women were too preoccupied to notice. Men were practically elbow to elbow inside the cantina making it almost impossible for Alvin to survey the crowd for the three men he was after. So, after pausing for just a few seconds inside the doorway, he began making his way through the crowd to the bar. The same bartender and a woman young enough to be his daughter were behind the bar doing their best to keep up with the men barking at them for tequila.

"Great place for a pickpocket," Alvin thought to himself, placing a hand over his watch and chain as he continued making his way through the crowd.

Alvin was still trying to inch his way toward the bar when the already noisy cantina became even louder and all eyes turned toward the door as two Mexican man entered holding roosters high above their heads. As the crowd surged toward the two men so that everyone could get a better look at the roosters, Alvin managed to make his way to the bar and when the young woman spotted him, she tossed her long black hair behind her shoulders and made her way to his end of the bar.

"Tequila, Señor?" she asked with a seductive smile.

"Si," Alvin replied smiling back.

"Are you here for the cock fights, Señor?"

"I guess so. I never been to one before. So, maybe you could help me pick a winner," Alvin replied in a flirting tone.

"Maybe so," she said as she sat a brown porcelain shot glass on the bar and filled it with tequila. "There are many men who say I bring them luck."

"Well, I could sure use some of that," Alvin chuckled and then emptied the glass.

"Another, Señor?"

"Sure why not," Alvin said smiling and looking into her deep brown eyes. "I'd offer to buy you a drink, but I'm not sure you're old enough to drink," Alvin added with a teasing grin.

"I am old enough, Señor," she replied with the same seductive smile. Then after refilling the glass she added, "I am old enough for many things."

As Alvin reached for the glass, she placed her hand over his stopping him short. His eye brows lifted as she downed the tequila, licked the inside of the glass, and then placed it back on the bar without ever taking her eyes off of him.

"Would you like some more, Señor?" She asked as she slowly pulled the scooped neckline of her blouse down a few inches with her thumb.

"Are we still talking about tequila or..."

"Whatever you like, Señor," she replied as Alvin's voice trailed off.

"Well, I reckon I better hold off at least until after the cock fights are over. Best keep my wits about me if I'm gonna be bettin' money on one of those roosters," Alvin said with a trace of uneasiness in his voice.

"Maybe later," she replied after a soft laugh. "Maybe later we could get together, drink some more tequila, and get to know each better."

"Well, it sounds like things are about to start. So I reckon I better get out there," Alvin replied as he laid a silver dollar on the bar and turned toward the door.

"Bet on the black one, Señor!" She said loudly as Alvin started following the crowd that was making its way outside.

Alvin paused and turned to face the young woman.

"The black one," Alvin replied smiling "Okay...I'll do that."

In the wide alley next to the cantina, the crowd formed a circle around a ring of kerosene lanterns that were already set out on the ground. Two men representing the owners were in the ring collecting money from the men and women in the crowd that were shouting out their bets while the owners were in the middle of the ring holding their roosters face to face, trying to antagonize, and provoke them into what would be a fight to the death. Alvin slowly moved around the outside of the crowd carefully studying the men on the opposite side of the ring. He stopped suddenly when he spotted a tall man in the crowd wearing a black hat with a silver concho hat band. Beside him was a much shorter, bearded man who was holding a fist full of money over his head and yelling at the top of his lungs, trying to get the attention of the men taking bets. Alvin continued to scan the crowd looking for the other tall man with the scar on his cheek, but he was not in the crowd. Alvin turned his attention back to the other two men and began comparing their features to the description of stage robbers he had stored away in his mind. A smile crossed his face as he became convinced that these were two of the three men he was after and his thoughts turned to planning their apprehension. A moment later the crowd erupted into near chaos as the two feathered gladiators were thrust at each other for one final time and then released to begin their fight to the bitter end.

 From where Alvin stood, he caught only an occasional glimpse of the two roosters that were battling for the right to live and fight another day. The poor vantage point actually suited Alvin just fine because he didn't hold with cruelty to animals and he considered cock fighting barbaric. But, others in the crowd were of a different opinion. A few shoving matches and even brief fist fights broke out among the spectators as the feathers continued to fly and people tried to maintain their view of the fighting cocks. After several minutes of pecking and clawing at each other, the fight between the two roosters ended with the battered and bloodied rusty colored rooster collapsing, while the nearly black one continued pecking and tearing flesh from his dead opponent. Several more fist fights broke out in the crowd as the men holding the money tried to sort out the winners from the losers and determine how much money was owed. Then suddenly the fisticuffs turned into a knife fight. The fight ended almost as quickly as it had started, but not before several men were cut and another stabbed several times. The crowd started to disperse as friends and relatives cared for those with minor wounds and the cantina became crowded again once the seriously injured man was carried away. Alvin watched the two men collect their winnings and then he followed them into the cantina. The two men made their way to the bar, but Alvin remained close to the door where he would be sure to see the men when they left. The two men talked and joked with the other men at the bar while drinking shots of tequila and flirting with the young woman who kept their attention with suggestive comments as she took their money and refilled their glasses. After several minutes and several shots of tequila, the short bearded man and a man that had been beside him at the bar staggered toward the door leaving the tall man behind. Alvin decided to follow the short man hoping that he would lead him to the third man or to wherever it was that they stayed when they were in Jal. The two men walked past several buildings on the main street and Alvin lost sight of them momentarily as they turned down an even darker side street, but they quickly reappeared when they walked onto the porch of an adobe with a red globed kerosene lantern hanging on the wall next to the brightly painted red door. Drunken laughter filled the street as the two men pounded on the door while calling out the names of two women. When the door opened, Alvin caught a glimpse of a scantily clad woman standing in the doorway. She invited the men inside and then closed the door behind her. Within minutes, faint shafts of light streaked through the bedroom windows on both sides of the adobe. Alvin made his way to the only window on the front of the building and peered through the dingy glass. The thin red curtains offered little privacy and Alvin quickly saw that the front room was empty. Alvin studied the room trying to get a general feeling for the floor plan of the adobe. On the opposite wall was a narrow open archway with strands of beads draped from the header. On each side of the archway was a door behind which Alvin assumed were bedrooms. The doors were closed, but Alvin could see a dim streak of light below each door. Alvin moved to the front door and pulled his pistol as he tried the door knob. It was locked. Alvin left the front of the adobe and quietly walked around to the east side of the building. With his pistol still ready, he put his back to the wall and inched his way toward the dimly lit window. The annoying sound of a barking dog, a few houses away, drowned out the squeaking bed springs, laughter, and giggles coming from inside until Alvin was right beside the window. He dropped down to his knees and peeked through the lower corner of the glass. In the gap between the curtains and window frame, he could see the short, bearded man trying to get the most for his two dollars. Alvin ducked under the window and crept toward the rear of the house hoping to find a back door. When he spotted the door, he gingerly made his way across the rickety wooden porch and peered through the window in the door. On the far side of the dark kitchen, Alvin could see the strands of beads hanging across the arched opening that led into the front room. Alvin slowly tried the door knob and it turned without resistance. He quietly opened the door and stepped inside closing the door behind him. The faint sounds of squeaking bedsprings, heavy breathing, and giggles coming from within the thin walled bedrooms were sure signs that his entry had not been heard. Alvin took a deep breath hoping to calm his racing heart and ever so slowly began creeping across the kitchen with his eyes trained on the beaded doorway. A sudden blood curdling screech pierced Alvin's ears. His heart skipped a beat and he jumped to the side as he felt something underfoot. Pots and pans hit the floor with a loud crash as Alvin ricocheted off of the cook stove. Then a cat darted past the silhouette of a man that had suddenly appeared in the beaded archway with a gun in his hand. Alvin instinctively fired his pistol. The man staggered backwards and fell over with a loud thud. Alvin rushed through the strands of beads anxious to see which man he had shot and quickly discovered that the man lying on the floor, in a puddle of blood, wearing only his socks was not the man he was hoping for. Alvin quickly moved to the door in the right corner of the room, jerked it open, and burst into the room ready to fire his pistol. The two dollar whore screamed and terror filled her eyes. Alvin scanned the room, but the short man was nowhere to be seen and when Alvin spotted the open window he knew why. The whore cried and begged Alvin not to shoot her as he hurried to the window and peered into the dark night, but the short man was long gone. Then a shot rang out and Alvin felt a burning sensation in the back of his left shoulder. He spun around and when Alvin saw that the whore was holding a small two shot derringer, he instinctively fired his pistol. The whore fell back unto the bed and the sheets quickly turned red as blood drained from the gaping .45 caliber hole in her chest.

"Son of a bitch!" Alvin cursed as he stared at the dead woman.

The whore, who had been with the other man, appeared in the doorway, naked to the waist. She screamed as she saw her dead sister on the bed. Alvin glanced at her with panicked eyes. Then he holstered his pistol and quickly disappeared through the open window.

Alvin ran away from the house and continued running until he was well past the last building in town. He took refuge in a shallow dry wash to catch his breath and quickly looked back toward the town to see if he was being followed. As he lay there still panting, he probed the front of his left shoulder hoping to find that the bullet had passed through causing relatively little damage. After finding no exit wound, he tried probing the back of his shoulder. He could feel the shirt starting to stick to his skin as the blood began to coagulate and his fingers grew sticky as he continued trying to probe for the bullet hole, but the wound was out of his reach. Alvin remained in the dry wash watching the town which had become alive with activity as word of the shootings spread. His shoulder continued to stiffen, but the pain began to lessen somewhat as the damaged nerves started to become numb. After several hours, the town became quiet again and became increasingly dark as the residents of Jal grew tired and went to bed. It was after midnight when Alvin left the wash and made his way around the edge of town to the stable. Once his horse was saddled, he led it to the back stairs of the hotel and after retrieving his saddlebags and rifle, Alvin rode out of town.

When he reached Kermit, Alvin turned west toward Mentone without stopping. Although, Monahans was much closer and there was a doctor in town, Alvin knew there would be a lot of questions asked about his gunshot wound, and he needed time to think. So, he decided to ride to the Double M ranch. It was almost twenty fours later by the time he reached the ranch. He hadn't lost much blood, but the .22 caliber bullet that was still lodged in his shoulder was causing him considerable concern and he was running a fever. The bunk house was dark as was the main ranch house, but as he rode through the entrance to the ranch, Alvin could see a light on the backside of the main house coming from what he knew was Lucy's room. Alvin dismounted at the front of the house and after tying his horse to the hitching rail by the porch, he walked around to the back of the house. The thick curtains on her bedroom window prevented him from seeing Lucy who was sitting in front of the dresser mirror, brushing her hair. Alvin tapped lightly on the window as he quietly called out her name. The noise startled Lucy and she automatically went for the pistol in the nightstand by her bed, but she stopped when she heard her name.

"Who's out there?" she asked once she was by the window.

"It's me, Alvin."

"Alvin?!" she repeated as she parted the curtains and then raised the window. "What are you doing out there?"

"I saw your light and I didn't want to wake everyone, but I need some help."

"What's wrong?" she asked.

Before Alvin could reply, Lucy noticed the beads of sweat on his forehead and quickly touched his skin with the back of her hand.

"You're burning up with fever! Come around to kitchen and I'll let you in!"

Lucy met Alvin at the back door to the kitchen and once he was inside, she immediately noticed the dried blood on the back of his shirt.

"You're hurt!"

"Yeah, I'm afraid I've been shot."

"Shot...oh my god!" Lucy said with a shocked expression. "We need to get you to a doctor."

"No! No doctor!"

"Why not? That bullet has to come out!" Lucy said as she tried to inspect the bullet wound.

"It's a long story."

"But, that bullet has to come out. It's probably the reason you're running a fever."

"I was hoping maybe you could dig it out. I'm pretty sure it's just a small bullet. Probably a .22 caliber."

"Me?" Lucy asked with an even greater shocked expression and eyes the size of silver dollars. "I better go get, Mama!"

Lucy hurried out of the kitchen and returned in less than a minute with Willow trailing behind her still trying to put on her robe.

"Alvin, what on earth happened?" Willow asked after shaking the sleep from her head.

"I'm afraid I messed up, Willow. I followed a couple of wanted men into New Mexico. I ended up shooting a man and then a prostitute shot me."

"Okay, sit down and let me take a look at that shoulder," Willow ordered. Then turning to Lucy she said, "Go wake Luke up and tell him to hitch up the wagon. We've got to get Alvin to the doctor."

"I can't go to a doctor, Willow."

"Why not? This bullet has to come out before the wound gets infected or you get blood poisoning."

"Okay, but no doctor. If the Rangers find out how I got shot, I'll be in big trouble."

"Why is that?" Lucy asked.

"Because... I had no business being in New Mexico. It's out of my jurisdiction. Besides that, I had no business being in that house where I shot that man and the prostitute. They had no idea I was a Ranger."

"Alright Alvin, I guess I'll have to take that bullet out myself," Willow said with a displeased look. "Lucy, build a fire in the stove and boil some water. Then help Alvin get that shirt off while I go get a sheet that we can tear up and use for bandages."

Willow left the kitchen and returned a few minutes later with a cotton sheet, a leather belt, and the jug of whiskey from the hall tree.

"Better take a swig of this," she said as she sat the jug on the table in front of Alvin. "But first, let me get you a glass, so you don't have to strain your shoulder."

"Thanks, Willow. I'm sorry to be such a bother," Alvin replied with sheepish eyes.

"Better hold your thanks and your apologies until after I get that bullet out," Willow said with a slight chuckle as she filled a glass with the amber liquid from the jug. "Once I go to digging that bullet out, you're liable to want to cuss me instead of thanking me."

Willow and Lucy tore the sheet into long strips and once the water was boiling, Willow poured off some of the water into a large wash pan to cool. Then after returning the pot to the stove, she placed a small paring knife and a hand towel in the boiling water. When the water in the wash pan had cooled to the point that she could stick her hands in it, she washed her hands with a bar of lye soap. Then she fished the hand towel out of the boiling water with a long wooden spoon and after letting it cool, Willow used it to clean in and around the bullet hole in Alvin's shoulder.

"Okay Alvin, better take another swig or two of that whiskey," Willow said as she refilled the glass from the jug.

Alvin took two sizable gulps from the glass and when he sat the empty glass on the table, Willow poured another two fingers into the glass and downed it herself.

"Mama!" Lucy said with a surprised look.

"You might think about taking a shot yourself," Willow said as she poured another two fingers in the glass and held it out to Lucy.

"Really, Mama!" Lucy said with raised eyebrows and a disapproving look.

"Don't get uppity with me, young lady. And don't pretend you never drank whiskey before either. You didn't really think I believed that story of yours when you came home after the last church social complaining of a headache. I could smell the whiskey on your breath!"

"Well you don't have to tell the whole world, Mama!" Lucy said with another shocked look.

When Lucy refused the glass, Willow emptied it in a single gulp, made another sour face, and set the glass aside.

"Lucy, you sit across from Alvin and hold both his hands. Try to keep his arms stretched out across the table and keep him from moving as best you can."

"Alright Mama," Lucy said with a worried look.

"I'm about to start cutting, Alvin. So, you best bite down on this belt," Willow said as she handed Alvin the belt.

Alvin smiled at Lucy and she smiled back as she took his hands and held them as tightly as she could. But their smiles quickly disappeared as Willow took the paring knife and started probing for the bullet. Alvin grimaced in pain and bit down on the belt to prevent himself from crying out. His face became flushed and his grip tightened like a vice on Lucy's hands as tears started to flow down his cheeks. Tears also flowed from Lucy's eyes, but she remained quiet without so much as a whimper, staring at Alvin, and pulling as hard as she could to keep him stretched out across the table. Beads of sweat started to form on Willows forehead and tears streaked down her cheeks as she realized how much pain she was inflicting, but her determination was unaffected.

"I got it," Willow said in a happy voice as she slid the bullet out of the wound on the tip of the knife.

Lucy smiled and released her grip of Alvin's hand as she felt his muscles relax. Alvin also smiled as he spit out the belt and sat up, but his face remained red as he wiped the tears from his cheeks.

"Here it is," Willow said holding up the small lead slug between her bloody fingers.

"Hard to believe such a small bullet could cause so much pain," Alvin said as he turned to see the bullet.

"Would you like some more whiskey," Lucy asked smiling at Alvin.

"I've probably had enough," Alvin replied with a weak a big grin. "That stuff is pretty stout and I'd hate to end up drunk on your kitchen floor."

"Maybe, I'll join you," Willow said laughing.

"Mama!" Lucy said in an astonished voice with another

disapproving stare.

"Oh Lucy, don't be so starched. I was only kidding," Willow said with an amused look.

After again cleaning the wound, Willow sewed a few stitches to close the incision. Then she and Lucy bandaged Alvin's shoulder and placed his arm in a sling.

"I guess that does it." Willow said with a long relieved sigh.

"I sure appreciate it, Willow."

"I know you do, Alvin," Willow said with a tired smile. "We'll, let's get you off to bed. Lucy, show Alvin to the spare bedroom."

Lucy helped Alvin to the spare bedroom while Willow tidied up the kitchen and shortly thereafter the house was again quiet.

Chapter Six

The following morning, Alvin was up before anyone else in the house. After dressing, he went to the kitchen, built a fire in the cook stove, and put a pot of coffee on. Then he walked outside and sat on the steps leaving the door open behind him. His shoulder was stiff and the flesh around the wound was swollen, but removing the bullet eased the pain significantly. The morning air was cool and calm for the moment, but Alvin knew the temperature would probably be in the mid-nineties by noon. Alvin turned to look back into the kitchen when he heard footsteps and then stood up when he saw Willow walking toward the door.

"Morning," Alvin replied blushing slightly with embarrassment.

"Good Morning, Alvin. How's your shoulder?"

"Much better, thanks. I sure am sorry for showing up like I did."

"Don't be silly. What good are friends if you can't depend on them in a time of need?"

"Well, I sure appreciate what you did for me."

"You're welcome, Alvin," Willow said in a soft voice."

"Smells like the coffee is done," Alvin said. "Would you like a cup?"

"Sit down. I'll get us both a cup and join you on the steps," Willow said. "We might as well enjoy the cool morning air while it lasts. I'm afraid it's going to be another hot day."

Alvin sat back down and Willow returned shortly with two cups of coffee.

"Mind If I ask you again what happened?" she asked as she handed Alvin a cup and then sat down beside him. "I know I asked you last night, but I guess I was still half asleep when you explained it."

"Well, I really crossed the line this time, Willow. I was after three men that robbed the stage coach outside of Peyote and killed the man riding shotgun. I knew they were headed for the New Mexico Territory, so I headed straight for Kermit and when I got there, I found out those men had been seen across the state line in a little town named Jal. I started to turn back which is what I should have done because I got no jurisdiction outside of Texas. But, it really riles me when outlaws get away with murder just because they cross some imaginary line drawn on a map. Anyway, I guess my anger sorta clouded my thinking and I rode on into Jal looking for those men. I found two of 'em in a cantina and when they split up, I followed one of them to... Well excuse me for saying so, but I followed the man to a whorehouse. I should have just waited for the man to come out, but instead... I snuck around to the back and went in through the kitchen. My plan was to apprehend the man and once I got his partners, I intended to bring all three of them back to Texas. Now that I think about it...it was a stupid plan, but like I said...I guess my anger got the best of me. Anyway, while I was making my way through the kitchen I stepped on a cat, knocked a pot off the stove, and the next thing I knew there was a man with a gun standing in front of me. It was dark and I couldn't see his face. All I saw was a man with a gun. So I shot him. Wouldn't have been too bad if it was the man I was after, but the man I shot turned out to be the wrong man. I guess he was just coming to see who was in the kitchen after I made all that noise. Anyway, by the time I got around to the bedroom where I had seen the man I was after, he'd already escaped through the window. And then the prostitute, he was with, shot me and...well...I shot her back. And then I came here for help... Never had to shoot a woman before," Alvin said in a sad voice with his head low and staring at the dirt.

As Willow listened to Alvin, she started to realize how much he had changed since the first time she met him some twelve years earlier. Outwardly except for the effects of time, the slight scar over his right eye, and the missing finger on his left hand, he hadn't changed much, but inside she sensed that Alvin had become a much harder and more cynical man with little tolerance and much less compassion for his fellow human beings.

"Well it does sound to me like you were just defending yourself, Alvin," Willow said once he finished telling the story.

"Yeah, but I had no right to be there in the first place and that man I shot, and the prostitute...they had no idea I was a Ranger.

They probably just figured I was a burglar or someone that come there to rob 'em. Folks got a right to defend themselves."

"So, what are your plans now, Alvin?"

"Well, I hate not finishing something once I've started it. So, I reckon I'll go back after those men. But I'll do it the right way...the legal way. And once I get 'em, I'm gonna quit the Rangers. Wouldn't be right for me to continue being a Ranger after what I done."

"I can't say I'm unhappy about you quitting the Rangers, Alvin. But, don't be so hard on yourself. After all...it was an accident."

"Yeah, but that's no excuse. What I did was wrong."

"Well, don't do anything until you've had a good chance to think about it," Willow said with a warm smile as she gently placed her hand on his. "But if you do decide to quit the Rangers, you've got a home and a job here anytime you want it."

"Thanks Willow," Alvin said with a weak smile as he looked into her eyes. "By the way, I'd appreciate it if you wouldn't tell Luke, or Duv, or any of the others about this."

"I won't and I'll make sure Lucy knows to keep quiet, too."

"Thanks, Willow."

"Well, I better start breakfast. The others will be up soon."

"Yeah, and I guess I better be on my way. Before anyone knows I'm here. Otherwise, they're sure to have a lot of questions once they see my shoulder all bandaged up."

"I suppose you're right. Take care of yourself, Alvin, and don't forget what I said. You can make this your home whenever you're ready," Willow said as she kissed Alvin on the cheek.

"Thanks, Willow. I might just take you up on that someday. Oh...and tell Lucy goodbye for me and tell her I said thanks, too."

"I will," Willow said with a curious smile.

Alvin left the Double M a few minutes later and rode back to Kermit by way of Mentone. When he arrived in Kermit, he checked into the hotel and early the next morning and each morning thereafter, Alvin was up with the sun. He rode out of town on the road to Jal and when he reached the stack of whitewashed rocks that served as the survey marker designating the Texas, New

Mexico line, Alvin led his horse to a rock outcropping about a quarter of a mile off the road where there was shade from the blistering sun and enough cover that he could keep an eye on the road without being seen. Alvin had a strong hunch that it was only a matter of time before the three stagecoach bandits would return to Texas to pull another job and he was determined to be there when they did. So, each time he spotted riders on the road, he spent considerable time surveying their features through his binoculars.

The days were long and the hours passed slowly. So, to amuse himself and help pass the time, Alvin practiced drawing against his shadow, throwing his knife, and he started keeping track of the number of men on the road by adding a pebble to a growing line in the dirt each time he raised his binoculars. On the second day, he added lifting rocks to his activities as a means of working the stiffness from his injured shoulder and strengthening the shoulder muscles.

After repeating the routine for six days, his perseverance finally paid off. It was mid-morning when he spotted two riders coming his way from across the state line. They were the first travelers he had seen all day. His first reaction was no different than it had been on countless other sightings. But as the two men got closer and he could see that one of them was short and the other fairly tall, his heart started to race. He tossed the rock that he had been using to exercise his shoulder aside and scrambled to his horse for his binoculars which were still in his saddlebags. He quickly focused his binoculars on the tall man just as a flash of sunlight reflected off of the silver Concho hat band. Alvin shifted his binoculars to the shorter man and immediately recognized him.

"Where the hell is the third man?" Alvin asked himself with a disappointed expression.

As he continued watching the two men, shifting back and forth between them with his binoculars, his mind filled with questions and possible explanations for the third man's absence. Although he was hoping to nab all three of the men, after giving it some thought, a grin stretched across his face.

"I guess two is a pretty good start...better than none," he said to himself.

As the two men rode past the stack of rocks marking the Texas state line, Alvin slithered further down into the crevice he was lying in to ensure he was not spotted. And once their backs were to him, he occasionally peered over the surrounding boulders to check their progress until they were about two hundred yards beyond the stack of whitewashed rocks. Then Alvin stood up and hurried around to the back side of the outcropping, untethered his horse, and swung up into the saddle. He started his horse loping after the two men trying to maintain enough distance from them so as not to alarm them, but close enough to keep them in sight through the rolling terrain.

When the two men reached the outskirts of Kermit, they slowed their horses to a walk and Alvin did the same. The two men pulled their horses to a stop in front of Hondo's Cantina, dismounted, and after tying their horses to the rough cedar hitching post, they went inside the cantina. Once the men were inside, Alvin hastened his horse's pace with his spurs and then reined him to a sudden stop when he reached the cantina. He dismounted quickly and tied his horse next to the others. His face was tight and expressionless, his eyes determined and set as he took his Ranger Badge out of his shirt pocket and pinned it prominently above his heart. He checked his pistol to ensure it would clear leather if needed and then walked toward the swinging doors of the cantina. He paused briefly at the doors and looked quickly around the smoke filled room. Three vaqueros at a corner table were drinking tequila, talking, laughing, and smoking cheap cigars. Two shabbily dressed cowboys with crumpled, sweat stained, hats sat at a table across the room, sharing a bottle and reminiscing about the good old days. The tall and short man were at the bar talking to Hondo as he poured them two whiskeys.

The hinges groaned as Alvin parted the swinging doors and stepped inside with his cold grey eyes locked on the men at the bar. Hondo's eyes grew wide and whiskey spilled onto the bar when he spotted Alvin. The two men sensed Hondo's uneasiness and quickly turned around to determine the reason for his concern. Alvin could see the fear that suddenly showed on the short man's face when he spotted Alvin's badge, but the tall man's face was blank, his eyes dark beneath the brim of his black hat. Only the jingle of Alvin's spurs broke the dead silence that suddenly fell over the cantina when the vaqueros and the two cowboys spotted Alvin's badge.

"You're both under arrest for robbery and murder!" Alvin said calmly, but in a loud authoritative voice as he stopped about a dozen yards short of the bar.

The short man remained motionless, his fear now very obvious on his face. Alvin focused on the tall man looking him directly in the eyes, knowing full well what was about to happen as the man's left hand slowly moved toward his fancy black holster rig. The man blinked and in a split second both he and Alvin went for their guns. Two deafening shots rang out almost simultaneously and then another and another as the tall man was thrown back against the bar by Alvin's bullets. The man's eyes rolled back in his head and his mouth hung open as he slid off the bar like a wet dish towel. Alvin instantly turned his attention and his colt to the short man, who was crouching down on one knee at the base of the bar. Alvin mechanically cocked his Colt and aimed it at the man's head. His trigger finger seemed to tighten on its own.

"Don't shoot, don't shoot!" the man begged with his hands shielding his face.

Alvin's trigger finger suddenly relaxed and the rest of the saloon seemed to come into focus. He glanced at Hondo who was backing away with his hands in the air. He looked quickly at the vaqueros and then the two cowboys.

"It's over," he thought to himself as he looked back at the short man who was still cowering on the floor at the base of the bar.

Alvin let out a long sigh as he lowered the hammer on his colt and holstered it.

"Keep your hands up," Alvin said as he bent over, pulled the man's pistol, and stuck it in his belt. Then jerking the man to his feet he said calmly, "Okay let's go."

"Who's going to clean up this mess and what about him?" Hondo shouted pointing at the tall man's body lying on the floor in a growing pool of blood.

"The money you get for his horse, saddle, and gun aughta

cover it. If not... send the State of Texas a bill," Alvin replied in an uncaring voice as he continued prodding the short man toward the door.

Once they were outside the cantina, Alvin got a pair of handcuffs from his saddlebags and clamped them on his prisoner's wrists.

"Get on your horse," Alvin said holding the reins. "But, I'm warning you...you try riding off and I'll put a bullet in your back!"

Alvin mounted his own horse and with his prisoner's horse in tow, he started toward Monahans. As they passed the un-kept cemetery on the outskirts of town, Alvin noticed the two new graves. A remorseful frown appeared on his face and his eyes became fixed on the two fresh mounds of dirt.

"Can I ask your name?" the prisoner asked breaking Alvin's stare.

"Yep, I'm Alvin Witherspoon...What's yours?"

"Brady Hines."

"What about the other fella? What was his name?"

"Dean Stuckey," Brady replied.

"What happened to your other partner?"

"I don't know what you're talking about," Brady replied in an uneasy voice.

"No sense lying, Brady. There were three of you that were in on those stage hold ups outside of Peyote. And there were three of you when you killed the shotgun guard. Stuckey's already dead. You'll hang for murder and so will that third man, eventually. It's only a matter of time."

"Wasn't me that killed that guard."

"Doesn't really matter who pulled the trigger. You were there and you were involved in the hold up. So, according to the law, you're all equally guilty. The only thing that might save you from a hangman's noose is if you cooperated and helped us catch that third man."

About an hour passed with nothing more said between Alvin and Brady as they continued down the dusty road toward Monahans.

"Where are you taking me?" Brady asked, breaking the long

silence.

"Monahans," Alvin replied in a matter of fact voice.

"Then what?"

"I'm gonna turn you over to the sheriff. He'll hold you for trial and then you'll be hanged."

"What if I do like you said? You know... cooperate. Will you turn me loose?"

"Nope, I'll still hand you over to the sheriff and you'll still stand trial. The only difference is you'll go to prison instead of the gallows."

"How long will I go to prison for?"

"That'll be up to the judge?"

"Well, I reckon going back prison ain't so bad."

"Sounds like you been there." Alvin said.

"Yeah, I spent four years in Huntsville for rustling."

"How long ago did you get out?" Alvin asked only slightly surprised.

"Got out in December."

"Didn't take you long to get back on the wrong side of the law," Alvin said after a short chuckle.

"Well, things just didn't go the way I planned them. I was hoping to get a job on a ranch somewhere. But, I ended up tagging along with Dean and Pete. After we held up that stage the first time and I saw how easy it was, I guess I just got caught up in it." Brady said in a depressed tone. "This was gonna be our last job. Me and Dean was gonna head for Mexico after just one more hold up."

"Was you and Dean in Huntsville together?"

"Yeah, we was cell mates."

"What about that other fella...Pete? Was he the third man on the hold ups?"

Brady remained silent for a minute, mentally retracing what he had said, not realizing that he had mentioned Pete's name.

"What about it?" Alvin asked looking Brady in the eyes.

"Yeah, I guess you'll find out anyway. He was our other cell mate. We all met up in Odessa once Pete got out?"

"What was Pete's last name?"

"Weston," Brady replied without hesitation

"What was he in for?"

"I'm not sure. He never would talk about it. But, it must have been pretty serious because he was serving a fifteen year sentence. But, he got out a couple years early for good behavior."

"Weston...Pete Weston...seems like I've heard that name somewhere," Alvin said, his forehead wrinkled in thought.

"Where is Weston now?"

"If I tell you, will you put in a good word for me to the judge...you know for cooperating? If you'll do that, I'll also tell you who pulled the trigger on that shotgun guard...and I promise you it wasn't me."

"Alright, you have my word on it, but you better be telling the truth. I find out you lied...and you'll go straight to the gallows."

"It was Pete that killed the guard. That's why he went his own way after we got back to New Mexico. Me and Dean stayed in Jal, but Pete kept on going."

"Where was he headed?"

"Alamogordo," Pete replied. "Said he had a brother that lives there."

"Now I remember!" Alvin said with a surprised look. "Pete Weston is the fella that stole a bunch of money from a rancher, kidnaped his wife, and left her for dead about twelve years ago!"

"You don't say?" Brady replied with an equally surprised look.

"How long ago did Weston get out of Huntsville?"

"Back in January, sometime."

"That when the three of you met up in Odessa?"

"No, we didn't get together until about a month later."

"Any idea where Weston was between the time he got out of Huntsville and the day he met up with you and Stuckey in Odessa?'

"I don't believe he ever said and Pete's not the kinda fella you press for information. Me and Dean just figured he had something he needed to take care of."

"Yeah, and I gotta hunch I know what that was!" Alvin said as he put the spurs to his horse.

It was well after dark by the time Alvin arrived in Monahans. Once Brady Hines was locked up in a jail cell, Alvin provided

Sheriff Joe Mortise with the details surrounding the death of Dean Stuckey and everything he knew about Pete Weston, including his suspicion that Pete Weston was responsible for killing Punch Masters.

Once Alvin was finished explaining everything to the sheriff, he spent several minutes putting it all down on paper to serve as his official report.

"You want me to see that it gets on tomorrow's stage to Odessa?" the sheriff asked when he noticed Alvin folding the report.

"Yeah thanks, Joe."

"I'll have the misses set another place at the table if you want to join us for supper."

"Thanks Joe, I appreciate the invite, but I got a few things I need to take care of before morning. So, I believe I'll pass, but give my regards to Sue Ellen."

After leaving the sheriff's office, Alvin walked to the telegraph office.

"Howdy Ranger, what can I do fer you?" the telegraph operator asked Alvin as he entered.

"I'd like to send a telegram to the prison warden over in Huntsville."

"You betchya. Just write out your message and I'll send it right out."

Alvin wrote out his message and handed it to the telegraph operator.

"I'll send it right out, but I doubt you'll get a response before morning," the telegrapher said after reading the message.

"That's fine. I'll check back in the morning," Alvin replied.

Alvin left the telegraph office and walked back to the sheriff's office for his and Brady's horses. Then he led the horses to the stable and after arranging for their keep, he walked to the hotel. Once his gear was stowed in his room, Alvin had dinner in a cafe not far from the hotel. On his way back to the hotel, Alvin stopped in at the saloon, where he bought a bottle of whiskey before returning to his hotel room.

Alvin sat on the edge of his bed, deep in thought, occasionally glancing at the bottle of rye whiskey at his feet, but refusing to open it. After several minutes, he retrieved a pencil and paper from his saddlebag and started writing out a letter of resignation from the Rangers. It was a bitter sweet moment when he signed the letter, but by his own admission, the decision was one that was long past due. Alvin folded the letter and placed it on the wooden box that served as a nightstand. Then he uncorked the bottle of rye and held it up above his head as he said, "To the Texas Rangers!"

As he thought about the good times, the bad times, and his experiences in general over the past sixteen years, Alvin continued drinking from the bottle until it was about half empty and the details of his accomplishments as a Ranger became clouded. At which point, Alvin replaced the cork in the bottle, removed his Ranger Badge, placed it on top of the letter, and fell back on the bed.

The following morning, Alvin woke still lying on the bed fully dressed. He got out of bed, shaved, and after washing his face; he put on a clean shirt, gathered up his things, and walked to the telegraph office. The telegraph operator greeted him in the same manner as he had the night before and then quickly handed Alvin the reply to his telegraph. Alvin's jaw tightened as he read the telegram which confirmed that Pete Weston had been released from prison two weeks prior to Punch's murder.

"By the way, you forgot to pin your badge on, Ranger," the telegraph operator said in a friendly voice.

"Thanks, but I didn't forget," Alvin said as he started for the door.

Alvin walked to the stable, and after saddling his horse, and strapping on his saddlebags, he rode to the jail. The sheriff and his deputy were looking through the latest wanted posters and drinking black coffee when Alvin entered the office.

"Mornin' Alvin," the sheriff and deputy said almost in unison.

"Mornin' fellas," Alvin replied with a big smile.

"Help yourself to some of Tom's hot mud if you like," Joe said, motioning toward the coffee pot that was perched on top of the potbellied stove.

"Thanks, but strong coffee kinda sours my stomach. Besides I gotta get going."

"You ain't going after that Weston fellar are you?"

"Yep."

"I thought you said he was out in the New Mexico Territory somewheres."

"That's right, so I got a favor to ask. This here is my letter of resignation from the Rangers," Alvin said with a weak smile as he laid the envelope on the sheriff's desk.

"Resignation?" the sheriff said with a shocked look. "You mean after all these years you're gonna quit the Rangers? Just like that?"

"Yep, so I'd appreciate it if you would see to it that this envelope gets mailed to the Ranger Outpost in Odessa. And I'm gonna leave my badge with you for safe keeping. I imagine the Rangers will send somebody down to collect it in a day or two after they get my letter," Alvin said as he pulled his badge from his pocket and placed it on top of the envelope. "I'm gonna hang onto my Colt, my Winchester, and my horse. The Rangers can deduct what they're worth from my back pay. It's all explained in my letter."

"You resigning just to go after that Weston fellar?" Tom, the deputy, asked.

"That's some of it... but not all of it," Alvin replied with another weak smile. "Weston just helped me make up my mind. Mostly I'm quitting the Rangers...because it's time... that's all. It's just time."

"Well, good luck to you, Alvin. The Rangers are losing a good man!" the sheriff said as he got up from his chair.

Alvin shook hands with the sheriff and his deputy. Then he left their office, mounted his horse, and headed southwest toward Pecos.

Chapter Seven

Luke, Duv, and all of the other Double M hands were busy working on Luke's new house when Alvin rode through the ranch entrance. He was nearly to the main ranch house before anyone spotted him and once Duv recognized him, he and Luke put down their hammers and walked out to greet him.

"Surprised to see you back here so soon," Duv called out as Alvin dismounted.

"How are you, Duv?" Alvin asked as he shook Duv's hand.

"Good to see you again," Luke said smiling as he and Alvin shook hands. "How come you ain't wearin' your badge?"

"Well, I ain't a Ranger no more...I resigned," Alvin said with a big smile.

"So, I guess that makes you just another saddle bum," Duv chuckled.

"I reckon so," Alvin said grinning at Duv.

"You ain't looking for a job, are you?" Duv asked with a hopeful look.

"Not exactly," Alvin replied.

"What brings you out this way then?" Luke asked with a puzzled look.

"I think I know who shot your father, Luke."

"You do?" Luke asked with a stunned look.

"Who was it?" Duv asked with an equally surprised look.

"You remember, Pete Weston?"

"The man that stole Punch's money and kidnapped Willow?" Duv asked looking even more stunned.

"Yep, that's him."

"I figured he was still in prison," Duv replied.

"He got out in January."

"I'll be damned! I wish Punch would have just let me shoot him like I wanted too!"

"What makes you think it was him that shot my pa?"

"You fellas hear anything about the stagecoach robberies that happened over by Peyote?"

"Yeah, it was on the front page of the Pecos Gazette," Luke

replied. "Remember Duv, it was on that newspaper I brought back last week after Mary and I got back from visiting her father,"

"Yeah, I remember. The article said they killed the shotgun guard during the last hold up."

"Well, I caught up with two of the men that pulled off that robbery. I had to shoot one of 'em, but I arrested the other one. Anyway, the one I arrested told me the third man that was in on those holdups was Pete Weston."

"Well, I'll be damned! He kept saying he would get even with Punch the whole time we was taking him back to El Paso. I'd forgotten all about it. And I bet Punch did too," Duv said shaking his head in amazement. "Any idea where Weston is now?"

"New Mexico Territory according to that man I arrested."

"You think he's telling the truth?"

"If he ain't...he knows he'll hang," Alvin replied in a firm voice. "Anyway, I thought you fellas would want to know and I guess I aughta tell Willow, too."

"You plan on going after Weston?"

"Yep."

"That the reason you quit the Rangers? So, you could go after him?" Luke asked.

"That's part of it. But like I said last time we talked, it was time for me to leave the Rangers."

"Where you gonna start looking?" Duv asked.

"According to that man I arrested, Weston was heading for Alamogordo."

"That's the same place, me and Punch caught up with him," Duv said still showing his surprise. "He's got a brother that lives near there."

"Could I ride with you?" Luke asked.

"No offense, Luke, but this ain't a job for someone without experience. Weston is a killer of the worst kind, a back shooter, and he knows if he's caught...he'll hang. So, it won't be easy to take him. Besides, you got a ranch and a new wife to look after."

"Yeah, I guess you're right," Luke agreed in a disappointed tone. "I just figured since it was my pa he killed...Well, it just don't seem right for you to go risking your life without..."

"What if I went in your place, Luke?" Duv interrupted. "You can manage things without me for a while."

"I'm not so sure that's a good idea, Duv," Alvin said.

"I got as big a score to settle with Weston as you or anybody else, Alvin. And you know I can take care of myself," Duv said in a determined voice. "Besides that, when it comes to killing experience...I got plenty of that, too."

"I ain't doubting your ability, Duv. I haven't forgotten about what you did down along the Rio Grande... But, you got a wife and family to think about now."

"Yeah well, I ain't planning on gettin' killed," Duv replied looking Alvin in the eyes. "And I figure with the two of us after Weston, the chance of either of us getting hurt is pretty slim."

"Alright then, I guess it's only fair to tell you...I intend to kill Weston if I get the chance. I ain't bringing him back alive."

"Suits me just fine," Duv replied.

"Okay Duv, if that's the way you feel, I'd be a fool to say no."

"How about it, Luke? You okay with me taking some time off to go with Alvin?" Duv asked looking at Luke with the same determined expression.

"I guess so, Duv. But I still think, I aughta be the one to go."

"I know how you feel, Luke. But one of us has to stay here," Duv said.

"Besides that...Willow would never forgive me if I let you come along. You know that, Luke," Alvin added, smiling.

"Yeah, I guess so," Luke agreed with a soft chuckle

"When were you planning to start out, Alvin?" Duv asked with a hint of enthusiasm showing in his eyes.

"Well, I'd like to spend a few minutes with Willow, but we still got several hours of daylight. So after I finish talkin' to Willow...I was planning on hittin' the road."

"Okay, I'll go gather my things. I can be ready as soon as you are."

While Luke took Alvin up to the main house, Duv went to his own house to gather his gear and say good bye to his wife and two boys.

"We got company," Luke announced as he and Alvin entered

the parlor.

Lucy walked out of the kitchen and her face beamed with delight as her eyes met Alvin's.

"Ranger Alvin Witherspoon!" she said as she dried her hands on her apron and hurried across the parlor.

"I'm afraid it's just plain Alvin, now... Lucy," Alvin said smiling and fidgeting with his hat. "I quit the Rangers two days ago."

"Good for you," Lucy said with an even bigger smile as she gave Alvin a hug.

"Where's Aunt Willow?" Luke asked.

"She's out back in the garden. I was just washing up some carrots," Lucy replied as she threaded her arm through Alvin's and started leading him toward the kitchen. "Mama will be glad to see you. How's your shoulder?"

"Fine, it's nearly all healed up."

"What was wrong with your shoulder?" Luke asked as he followed Alvin and Lucy to the kitchen.

"Oh...ah, I just hurt it a few weeks back."

"Mama, look who's here!" Lucy said loudly as she and Alvin walked out the back door.

"Why Alvin, what a pleasant surprise!" Willow said with a warm smile. "How's your shoulder?"

"How come everyone knows about his shoulder except me?" Luke asked Lucy with a puzzled look.

"You must have been too busy mooning over Mary, when he told us about it," Lucy replied in a teasing voice.

"I don't moon over her!" Luke said in a defensive tone. "We're just in love. Maybe you should try it sometime."

"Maybe I will," Lucy said with a sassy smile.

Willow removed her gardening gloves and gave Alvin a hug. She noticed the two pin holes above his left pocket and the absence of his badge, but she didn't mention it. Asking instead, "What brings you to our part of Texas?"

"I've got some news, Willow."

"I hope it's good news," she chuckled.

"I'm not sure if it's good or bad, but I figured you would want to know it," Alvin said. "It's about Punch's murderer."

The sparkle in Willow's eyes and her smile were suddenly gone.

"I know who shot him," Alvin continued. "It was a man named Pete Weston."

"The man from El Paso?" Willow asked with a surprised look. "Are you sure? I thought he was in prison."

"He was released two weeks before Punch was murdered," Alvin said with a blank look.

"I can't believe it...after all these years... I just can't believe it," Willow said shaking her head.

"Well, he won't get away with it, Willow. I intend to go after him, Alvin said with the same blank look.

"You're not going alone, I hope!"

"Matter of fact, I told Duv he could go," Luke interjected quickly.

"Duv?" Willow exclaimed.

"I wanted to go, but Alvin wouldn't have me," Luke replied with a jesting smile.

"You're needed here," Alvin said quickly.

"I know...Anyway, Duv wanted to go and I said ...okay," Luke replied. Then looking at Willow he added, "I hope that's alright with you, Aunt Willow."

"Well, I certainly don't care for the idea of Alvin going alone," Willow replied. Then turning to Alvin she asked, "Why can't you get help from the sheriff or more Rangers? Why does Duv need to be the one to go?"

"Weston is in New Mexico, Willow. Texas lawmen have no authority there," Alvin explained.

"Is that why you aren't wearing your badge?"

"I resigned from the Rangers, Willow."

"Just so you could go after Punch's killer?"

"You know I been thinking of resigning," Alvin said smiling. "Finding out about Pete Weston just forced my hand."

"Well, it sounds like your mind is all made up," Willow said with a worried look. "So, I guess there isn't much more I can say. Just promise me you'll be careful."

"I will and once I get him...I'll be back."

"Make him promise, Mama!" Lucy said smiling, but with worried eyes.

Alvin looked at Lucy and then back at Willow as he said, "I'll be back...I promise!"

Willow and Lucy tried to talk Alvin into staying the night, but Alvin was anxious to get started. So after a few hugs and handshakes, Alvin and Duv started toward New Mexico.

Chapter Eight

Days before Alvin ever confronted Pete Weston's partners in Kermit; Pete was already at his brother's ranch outside of Alamogordo. When he first rode up to his brother's house, the little girl playing in the front yard, stopped, and stared at the stranger.

"You must be Susie," Pete said as he dismounted. "Do you know who I am?"

The girl's curly blonde locks swung freely as she shook her head without speaking.

"No, of course not. You were just a baby last time I saw you," Pete said smiling. "I'm your Uncle Pete."

"I didn't know I had an Uncle Pete," Susie replied.

"Well, I been away for quite a spell," Pete chuckled. "Are your mama or papa around?"

"Mama's in the kitchen."

"Would you go tell her Uncle Pete is here?"

Susie skipped her way around to the kitchen where her mother and older sister, Megan, were busy peeling potatoes.

"Mama, there's a man out front. He says he's my Uncle Pete," Susie said as she entered the kitchen.

Charlene's eyes grew wide and a stunned look appeared on her face. She quickly parted the kitchen curtains and when she saw Pete, she opened a drawer in the counter and pulled out an old Forehand and Wadsworth revolver.

"What's wrong, Mama?" Megan asked with a worried look.

"Nothing! You and your sister just stay put."

"But Mama..."

"Just do as I say!" Charlene said loudly.

Charlene held the pistol with both hands as she left the kitchen and quickly walked around the house.

"Why you're even prettier than I remember, Charlene!" Pete said loudly with a cocky smile.

"What are you doing here, Pete? Aren't you supposed to be in prison?" Charlene asked with an angry look as she raised the pistol.

"Whoa there, Charlene," Pete said with a surprised look. "Is this any way to greet your brother-in-law?"

"Why aren't you still in prison?"

"I got out early," Pete replied, venturing a slight grin.

"Did they let you out or did you break out?" Charlene asked in a hostile voice.

"They let me out early for good behavior. I got my release papers right here in my saddlebag if you don't believe me," Pete said as he opened his saddlebag and retrieved a folded piece of paper.

"What do you want here?"

"I did my time, Charlene. I came here to visit the only kin I got and try to start my life over. I know those things I did were wrong, but I've changed. Twelve years in Huntsville taught me a lesson. I'm a different man now. Come on Charlene...can't we put all that behind us?"

"Maybe, but only because you're Grant's brother. But I'm warning you...you better keep your distance. You lay one hand on me and I swear...I'll run you off at gun point."

"Like I said, Charlene, I'm a different man now," Pete said removing his hat and offering her his most convincing smile.

"Okay, put your horse in the barn and come on inside. I'll move Susie in with Megan and you can sleep in her room. Grant and the boys should be here soon."

"Thank you, Charlene," Pete said in a humble and appreciative manner.

Pete led his horse to the barn and after stripping off the saddle; he snuck back to the entrance and carefully peered outside to ensure no one could see him. Then he returned to his horse and removed the sack containing his share of the loot from the stage robberies along with a half pint of whiskey from his saddlebags. After quickly looking around the barn for a hiding place, he hid the sack and bottle behind one of the wooden feed cribs. Pete was just leaving the barn when he spotted his brother, Grant, and his two boys coming up the access road to the house with a wagon full of fence posts and spools of barbed wire. Grant's expression showed his surprise and displeasure as he pulled the team to a stop.

"Before you say anything, Grant...hear me out," Pete said when he saw Grant's face. "First of all, I was let out early for good behavior and I got a release paper to prove it. I know the things I did was wrong, but I paid for my mistakes. That's all behind me now. Twelve years in Huntsville Prison has changed me. All I'm asking is for you to give me a chance to start my life over."

Grant stared at Pete in silence for a few minutes as he considered what Pete had said. Then a slight smile appeared on his face as he climbed down from the wagon and extended his hand to Pete. Pete took his hand and shook it with an appreciative smile.

"Thank you, Grant. This means a lot to me!"

"Well, you're still my brother," Grant replied smiling. Then turning to his sons he said, "Boys, come say hello to your Uncle Pete. Pete, this is Tyler and that there is Cody."

"Good to see you again, boys," Pete said as he shook their hands. "You was both just little boys last time I saw you. And now you're both young men."

"Cody is sixteen and Tyler will be eighteen next month," Grant said.

"They're fine looking boys, Grant. I imagine they're both a real help to you around the place."

"Yeah, I'm real proud of both of them," Grant said still smiling.

"Grant, you and the boys hurry up and get the team put up. Supper will be ready in half an hour," Charlene shouted from the kitchen door.

"Alright, Dear!" Grant replied.

"I'll give you a hand," Pete offered quickly.

Once the team of mules was unhitched and turned out to graze with the horses, Pete returned to the kitchen while Grant and his sons washed up and brushed some of the road dust from their overalls. When Grant and his sons returned to the kitchen, they all sat down at the table and joined hands while Grant gave thanks.

"Where have you been all these years, Uncle Pete?" Tyler asked as he spooned out a heaping helping of mashed potatoes and then passed the bowl to Cody.

Grant and Charlene looked at each other with raised eye brows and then Charlene said, "Let your uncle eat, Ty. He's been in the saddle all day and I'm sure he's hungry."

"That's okay, Charlene. The boy's got a right to know," Pete said with a weak smile. "Truth is, Tyler...I been in prison. I made a few mistakes when I was younger. But, getting caught and sent to prison was the best thing that ever happened to me. I learned a lot in prison and I'm a better man for it."

"What did you do?" Cody asked with an astonished look.

"That's enough questions, Cody. Better eat your supper before it gets cold," Charlene said with a stern look.

"I'd like to answer the boy if you don't mind, Charlene," Pete said with puppy like eyes. "I ain't proud of the things I done, but I paid for my mistakes and my spending time in prison might be a good lesson for the boys."

Charlene nodded and Pete continued.

"I stole some money from a man and I kidnapped his wife, but I didn't mean her no harm. I just did it to keep him from coming after me," Pete said looking at the boys. "I was gonna let her go as soon as I got out of Texas."

"What's kidnapping?" Susie asked.

"That's when you make somebody go with you when they don't want to," Pete replied.

"Megan makes me go with her sometimes when I don't want to. Is that kidnapping?" Susie asked with an innocent look.

"I only make you go with me when mama tells me to," Megan replied in a defensive tone.

"So, how did you get caught?" Cody asked ignoring his sisters.

"Well, that woman...the man's wife, she fell off her horse and hit her head. Turns out she wasn't hurt bad, but the fall knocked her out. So, I had to leave her there. And when I did, her husband and another man came after me and when they caught me, I was sent to prison. So, take it from me fellas...do like the good book says and don't take nothin' that don't belong to you."

"What was it like being locked up in prison?" Tyler asked after gnawing off a row of corn and setting the stripped cob on his plate.

"That's enough, Tyler. This is not the proper conversation for the supper table," Charlene said giving both her sons and then Pete a stern look. "You can ask your Uncle Pete more questions when you're away from the table and away from your sisters."

"You're right, Charlene. I'm sorry," Pete said with an apologetic smile.

Later after everyone finished eating, Pete, Grant, and the boys went to sit on the front porch while Charlene and the girls washed the dishes and cleaned up the kitchen.

"Charlene don't allow me to drink in front of the girls, but I got a bottle stashed under the porch if you want a little nip before Charlene and the girls get through in the kitchen," Grant said as they were walking around the house.

"No thanks, Grant. I gave up whiskey."

"Brother, you really have changed!" Grant chuckled.

"Like I told you...twelve years in Huntsville made me a different man."

When they were settled on the front porch, Pete answered a few more questions about his prison experiences and then Grant took over the conversation talking mostly about the changing times. Charlene and the girls joined the men on the front porch, but the girls were whisked off to bed by Charlene a few minutes later and shortly thereafter everyone was off to bed.

The next morning after breakfast, while Charlene started home schooling Cody and the girls, Grant, Pete, and Tyler hitched up the wagon. After the three of them had one last cup of coffee, they clambered into the wagon and Grant drove it a few miles up the road to start fencing in the eighty acres he had recently bought from a widowed neighbor.

The days and evenings that followed varied little from that day forward except on Sunday when Pete attended church in Alamogordo with Grant and his family. It was only then that Charlene really started to believe that Pete had changed and her attitude toward him started to reflect her changing opinion.

Three weeks later, Charlene had just dismissed school for the day and was busy taking the linens she had washed earlier off of the clothes line. Cody was in the corral saddling the horse that he planned to ride over to where Grant, Pete, and Tyler were still working on the new fence and the girls were outside playing hide and seek around the barn. None of them was aware that Alvin and Duv had been up on a hill above the house keeping it under surveillance since they arrived shortly before noon.

"Don't look like anybody is around except the woman and the kids," Duv said as he handed the binoculars back to Alvin.

"Yeah, but let's wait awhile longer until we know why the boy is saddling that horse."

When Cody finished saddling the horse, he climbed up into the saddle and rode off to help with the fencing. Alvin and Duv remained on the hill until Cody was out of sight before returning to their own horses that were hidden in a stand of pinion on the back side of the hill.

"You really think that woman will tell us the truth when we ask her about, Pete?" Alvin asked Duv as he mounted his horse.

"I think so. Been a long time, but as I recall... she didn't seem the sort that would lie. In fact, I think she was about ready to shoot Pete herself once she found out what he'd done," Duv replied as he swung up into the saddle.

Charlene was on her way into the house with the basket of linens when she saw Alvin and Duv riding on the main road. She stopped to watch them and when she saw them turn off the road and continue toward the house, she set the basket on the ground and walked to the front of the house.

"Afternoon, Ma'am," Alvin said as he and Duv tipped their hats.

"What can I do for you, gentlemen?"

"We're looking for Pete Weston. We were told we could find him here." Alvin replied.

"Told by whom?" Charlene asked with a slightly worried look.

"It was a friend of his," Alvin replied.

"Do I know you?" Charlene asked staring at Duv. "You look familiar."

"Our paths crossed once," Duv replied.

"Is Pete wanted for something? Are you lawmen?" Charlene asked her voice trembling slightly.

"No Ma'am, we ain't the law," Alvin replied.

"Are you bounty hunters? Is that it?" Charlene asked, her

concern becoming more obvious.

"No Ma'am," Duv replied.

"Just tell us where we can find, Pete," Alvin said in a firm, impatient voice.

"We're not here to cause you or your family any grief, Ma'am. But we need you to tell us where Pete Weston is," Duv added in a more civil tone.

"I know who you are! You're one of the men that came after Pete when he stole that money!" Charlene said as she suddenly placed Duv's face.

"Yes, Ma'am."

"What has Pete done now?" Charlene asked as she tried to stop the tears from streaming down her cheeks.

"He robbed a stagecoach and killed two men," Duv replied.

"Are you sure it was, Pete?"

"We're sure, alright! And if you don't tell us where we can find him...we'll just wait here for him!" Alvin replied in a tone that reflected his impatience was turning to anger.

"Please, Ma'am...tell us where we can find him. So, we can deal with him away from you and your family," Duv said in a caring voice.

"He's out with my husband and my two boys building fence," Charlene replied tears now streaming from her eyes.

"Is that where the boy that just left was headed?" Alvin asked.

"Yes."

"How do we get to where they're building fences?" Alvin asked in a gentler tone.

"You go back the way you came for about a mile down the road. You'll be able to see the new fence posts and wire from the road."

"Alright, let's go, Duv." Alvin said.

"We appreciate the help, Ma'am," Duv said tipping his hat again.

"Please don't do anything that will endanger my boys or my husband!" Charlene begged.

"We won't," Duv said in a reassuring voice. "So if for some reason, we can't make our move today without putting your boys or husband in danger... we'd appreciate it if you wouldn't mention we were here."

"And if we don't get him today...don't forget we'll be watching the house," Alvin added.

"You have my word. I won't say anything. Just don't endanger Grant or my boys."

Duv nodded and gave Charlene a reassuring smile. Then he and Alvin rode off at a fast clip.

"Who were those men we saw riding away?" Susie asked as she and Megan walked toward Charlene.

"Oh, they were just a couple of strangers, asking for directions. I guess they were lost," Charlene said as she dried her eyes.

"Is something wrong, Mama?" Megan asked as she noticed the tears.

"No, nothing is wrong, sweetheart. I just turned my ankle. But, I'm alright now," Charlene replied forcing a smile.

Minutes before Cody left the house to join in the fence building project, Pete was swinging a pick trying to dislodge a stubborn rock that he had just struck with the clam shell posthole digger. The pick suddenly ricocheted off the rock hitting Pete's left leg, tearing his dungarees, and leaving a small, but deep gash in his leg. Grant and Tyler ran over to Pete when they heard him cry out in pain and saw him drop to the ground holding his leg.

"What happened?" Grant asked as he kneeled down next to Pete.

"Oh, the damn pick bounced off that rock and hit my leg," Pete replied as he pulled up his pant leg exposing the gash in his left calf.

"Don't look like it hit the bone," Grant said. Then turning to Tyler he said, "Tyler, go fetch the canteen from the wagon."

Tyler ran to the wagon and when he returned with the canteen, Grant poured water on Pete's leg to wash off the dirt and blood surrounding the wound.

"Don't look too bad," Grant said. "Can you stand on it?"

"Yeah, I think so. It ain't all that bad. Just stings some," Pete replied as Grant helped him to his feet.

"Well, we probably aughta get you back to the house and put some salve on it to keep that cut from getting infected," Grant said. "I'll have Tyler drive you back in the wagon."

"No need for that. Hell, I've had horse bites worse than this," Pete said after taking a few steps. "It'll be fine until we finish up and call it quits for the day,"

"Here comes Cody, Pa," Tyler said as he spotted his brother coming through the trees.

"Just in time," Grant said. "Pete, you can take Cody's horse and ride it back to the house."

"Nah, I'll be alright."

"Don't be stupid. Ride on back to the house and get Charlene to clean up that cut and put some salve on it," Grant insisted.

Pete was on his way back to the house, but still quite a distance away when he spotted two men riding away from the house. Although he had no way of knowing it was Alvin and Duv, the sight of the two men raised his suspicions and gave him an uneasy feeling. Pete's stomach started to churn as he pulled Cody's horse to a stop and continued watching the two men. When the men reached the road and turned in his direction, Pete quickly reined his horse off the road and rode into a nearby shallow wash that was surrounded by pinions. Then he quickly dismounted and placed his hand over the horse's muzzle to keep it quiet. As the two men rode by at a fast clip, Pete was sure he had seen one of the men before, but he couldn't remember where. His eyes continued to follow the two riders until they disappeared over a rise in the road. Then Pete mounted his horse and started it galloping toward the house.

Susie and Megan were jumping rope near the barn when Pete rode up.

"Where's your Mama?" Pete asked loudly as he quickly dismounted.

"She's inside. I don't think she's feeling very well," Megan replied as she stopped skipping rope.

"Would you girls take care of Cody's horse for me?"

"What happened to your leg?" Megan asked as she noticed Pete was limping slightly and saw the blood on his pant leg.

"I hit it with a pick," Pete replied. "So you girls stay outside while your mama doctors it."

Pete handed the reins to Megan and hurried to the back door. Charlene was sitting at the kitchen table with her face buried in her hands. She looked up quickly as the screen door slammed closed and her red swollen eyes grew to the size of saucers.

"Something bothering you?" Pete asked.

"I just don't feel well," Charlene said in a nervous voice as she stood up and rubbed her eyes. "Wha...what are you doing back?"

"A pick glanced off a rock and hit my leg," Pete replied with a suspicious look. "Grant sent me back here to have you to doctor it."

"Sit down and I'll see what I can do," Charlene said trying to force a smile to hide her nervousness.

Pete sat down with his eyes still fixed on Charlene as she went to the sink and pumped some water into a wash pan.

"Pull up your pant leg," she said as she returned with the pan of water, a clean wash rag, and soap.

"Any visitors today," Pete asked calmly as Charlene bent down and started to wash Pete's lower leg.

Charlene paused and her heart started to race. She stared at the floor to avoid eye contact as she resumed cleaning the dried blood from the bruised skin around the wound.

"No...uhh, not today," Charlene replied in an obviously nervous tone.

"Funny, I thought I saw a couple of riders leaving the house," Pete said his suspicions now confirmed.

"Oh...those weren't visitors," Charlene said with a short, nervous laugh while keeping her head down to avoid eye contact. "They were just a couple of men that stopped by asking for directions."

"Directions to where?" Pete asked, anger building inside of him.

"I'll get some salve to put on that cut," Charlene said as she stood up and started toward the counter.

Charlene reached for the drawer where she kept the Forehand and Wadsworth pistol, but before she could open it, Pete grabbed her from behind and threw her against the wall.

"They were looking for me weren't they?" Pete asked in a loud angry voice. "What did you tell them?"

"Nothing...I didn't tell them anything!" Charlene replied, her eyes full of fear.

"You lying bitch!" Pete shouted as he slapped Charlene with the back of his hand.

Charlene lunged for the drawer, but Pete grabbed her by the hair and pulled her back, throwing her against the wall again. Charlene tried to run to the door, but Pete grabbed her dress with his left hand and struck her again with the back of his right. Blood filled her mouth as his knuckles split her lip and then spewed out on the floor as she screamed. Pete threw her to the floor, tearing her dress and jumped on top of her. His eyes were glazed with anger as he continued tearing away her dress.

"Stop! Please stop!" Charlene screamed with her arms flailing as she tried to fight Pete off. "For god's sake...I'm your brother's wife!" she pleaded.

Pete's right hand moved to her throat as he lifted her dress. Charlene gasped for air, desperately clawing at his hand, but after twelve years of hard labor, Pete's grip was like the jaws of a steel trap. After a few seconds, Charlene's arms went limp from exhaustion and lack of air. Tears poured from her eyes, further clouding her vision, as she stared at the ceiling unable to scream or beg for Pete to stop raping her.

"I should have done that a long time ago," Pete said with a wicked laugh as he got to his feet and started buttoning his pants.

Pete left Charlene curled up on the kitchen floor, wheezing, and sobbing while he hurried to the bedroom and quickly gathered his things. When he returned to the kitchen, he bent over Charlene and said, "You probably would have enjoyed it, if you hadn't put up such a fight!" Then laughing, he added, "Adios, sister-in law!"

"Where you going, Uncle Pete?" Susie asked as Pete approached the barn where she and Megan were again skipping rope.

"I'm gonna take a little trip," Pete replied smiling. "Would you two sweethearts go catch my horse and bring him up here to the barn, so I can saddle him?"

"Okay, Uncle Pete."

"And hurry it up!" Pete added to hasten their pace.

While the girls ran to the pasture for his horse, Pete went into the barn for his saddle and to retrieve the sack of money he had hidden behind the feed bunk.

"Forgot all about you," he said as he retrieved the sack of money and spotted the whiskey bottle.

Pete guzzled the remaining whiskey and then tossed the bottle aside. After stuffing the money bag into his saddlebags, he carried his saddle and the rest of his gear to the barn entrance to wait for the girls to return with his horse.

"What happened to your face, Uncle Pete?" Megan asked as she returned leading Pete's horse and noticed the scratches and blood on his face.

"Just some scratches from the barbed wire, I reckon," Pete replied as he hastily saddled his horse.

"Want me to fetch you a wash rag from the kitchen?" Susie asked.

"No, you best stay outside for a while. Your Mama still ain't feeling too good."

"Are you leaving for good, Uncle Pete?" Megan asked as she realized that Pete was strapping all of his gear on the saddle.

Pete looked at Megan and then Susie without replying. A trace of remorse momentarily showed in his eyes as he gazed at their innocent faces, but quickly disappeared.

"Will you be back, Uncle Pete?" Megan asked with a confused look when Pete turned away without replying.

Pete remained silent as he lifted his injured leg with his hands and put his foot into the stirrup. The pain showed on his face as he put weight on the leg and pulled himself up onto the saddle. Then without so much as another glance at the girls, he put the spurs to his horse and galloped away.

Chapter Nine

Unaware that Pete had seen them, Alvin and Duv continued up the road until they came to where the new fence started and ran south away from the road. Alvin and Duv slowed their horses to a walk and pulled their Winchesters as they turned their horses off the road and started following the line of new posts. When they came to where the trees gave way to open grassland, they stopped their horses and after returning his rifle to the saddle scabbard, Alvin pulled the binoculars from his saddlebag and focused them on the three figures near the wagon at the far side of the open pasture.

"You see him?" Duv asked impatiently.

"Not sure. One of 'em looks like that boy we saw leaving the house; can't tell about the other two," Alvin replied, handing the binoculars to Duv.

"One of 'em might be Pete, but I remembered him as being taller. The other one is too young to be Pete," Duv said after looking at the three figures for a moment. "I'm thinking that might be Pete's brother."

"Wonder what happened to the horse that boy was riding?" Alvin asked.

"I don't know, but I sure don't see it anywhere," Duv said as he scanned the rest of the open field.

"Maybe Pete took it and rode over that hill yonder," Alvin replied.

"Reckon we aughta wait here for a few minutes to see if he shows back up?" Duv asked as he handed the binoculars back to Alvin.

"Might as well. Don't look like the others are going anywhere," Alvin replied as he took the binoculars.

While Alvin and Duv continued waiting at the edge of the tree line, Alvin scanned the surrounding area with his binoculars hoping to spot Pete.

"Let's ride on over there and have a talk with them," Alvin said after several minutes passed with no sight of Pete.

Alvin returned the binoculars to his saddlebag and after again pulling his Winchester, he and Alvin started their horses walking toward the wagon.

"Couple of men comin' our way, Pa," Tyler said loudly as he happened to look towards the trees after tamping the dirt around the post he had just set.

"They don't look familiar," Grant said after watching the men for a moment.

"Want me to get your gun from the wagon?" Cody asked.

"No, we're on our own land and we ain't done nothin'. So, we got no reason to suspect trouble."

"Howdy!" Grant called out once Alvin and Duv were within shouting distance. "What can I do for you fellars?"

"Your wife told us we could find Pete Weston out here," Duv replied loudly.

"You just missed him," Grant said with a friendly smile as he looked at Alvin and then after fixing his eyes on Duv, he asked, "Do I know you?"

"Where did he go?" Alvin asked before Duv could reply.

"He hurt his leg. Hit it with a pick. So, I sent him back to the house to have my wife take care of it," Grant said glancing at Alvin as he replied. Then turning his attention back to Duv, he asked. "I know you from somewhere, don't I?"

"We just came from your house and Pete wasn't there," Alvin said in a firm voice as Duv remained silent.

"Look Mister, I don't know what this is all about, but I'm tellin' you, Pete hurt his leg and he rode back to the house to get it taken care of. I'm surprised you didn't pass him on the road. Couldn't have been more than half an hour ago that he left."

"Is there another way back to the house?" Duv asked, breaking his silence for the first time.

"No, just the same road you fellas took to get here. Otherwise you'd have to cross a couple of fence lines," Grant replied starting to look concerned.

"You thinking what I'm thinking, Alvin?" Duv asked while looking at Alvin.

"Yeah, he must have seen us coming," Alvin replied as he turned his horse around sharply and started it galloping back toward the road with Duv following close behind him.

"Get in the wagon, boys!" Grant shouted as he ran to the wagon.

Once the boys were in the wagon, Grant slapped the mules with the reins as he yelled, "Get up there, mules!"

When Alvin and Duv reached the house, they reined their horses to a stop, drew their pistols, and dismounted on the run.

"Check the barn! I'll check the house!" Alvin yelled as he ran toward the kitchen door.

Susie and Megan were in the barn. They rushed to the open entrance when they heard the horses and commotion outside.

"Is Pete Weston here?" Duv asked them quickly.

"He left a little while ago," Megan replied with a scared look as Susie sought safety behind her.

When Alvin burst into the kitchen, Charlene was propped up against the stove, shaking uncontrollably, and clutching the shredded dress to her bare chest. She looked at Alvin with hollow eyes and a listless stare as he paused briefly and shouted, "Where's Pete?" When he received no response, Alvin hurried away to search the rest of the house.

Duv arrived in the kitchen moments later and he immediately saw Charlene still on the floor. He felt his throat tighten as he looked at her bruised and swollen face.

"My god!" he croaked as he holstered his pistol and started to remove his shirt to cover Charlene. "You'll be okay. You're safe now," Duv said softly as he knelt beside her and wrapped his shirt around her shoulders.

Charlene looked at Duv with grey listless eyes, but said nothing."

"He ain't here!" Alvin said loudly as he reappeared in the kitchen.

Duv glanced at Alvin and then quickly turned his attention back to Charlene.

"Let's go, Duv! He's getting away!" Alvin repeated as he hesitated by the back door. "Come on, Duv... leave her! We gotta get after Weston before he gets away!"

Alvin hurried out the door and seconds later, Duv heard the

thundering hoof beats of Alvin's horse galloping away.

"You'll be okay, Ma'am," Duv said practically in tears as he stood up. "Your husband is on his way."

Duv hurried to the door, pausing briefly to reassure her again, saying," You'll be okay!"

Duv ran to his horse, but before mounting it he called the two girls over.

"I want you girls to promise me you won't go into the kitchen," Duv said as he kneeled down so that he could look the girls in the eyes. "You stay out here and play. Your papa and brothers are on the way here. So, you stay out here and wait for them. Okay?"

"Okay," Megan replied shrugging her shoulders.

"Promise me, now."

"Okay, we promise," Megan replied with a puzzled look.

Duv mounted his horse and started it galloping after Alvin.

Alvin slowed his horse momentarily when he reached the road just long enough to search for fresh tracks. Then he started his horse galloping north across open country with Duv following close behind. The tracks led Alvin and Duv around the west side of Alamo Peak and then turned northeast toward Cloudcroft.

"Better rest our horses or we'll end up following him on foot," Duv said loudly.

Alvin nodded and reluctantly pulled his nearly worn out and lathered horse to a stop.

Duv dismounted and without saying another word, continued following the tracks on foot while leading his horse.

"Something eating you, Duv?" Alvin asked after a few silent moments.

"We shouldn't have just left that woman like we did, Alvin," Duv replied in an angry voice.

"She'll be okay," Alvin replied with no hint of emotions.

"That ain't the point. She was scared out of her wits. Did you see the marks and bruises on her throat? That bastard nearly killed her. She probably figured she was gonna die right there, alone in her damned kitchen. We should have stayed with her until her husband got there."

"And let Weston get even further ahead of us than he is now?

What good would that do?" Alvin asked in an irritated voice. "I didn't come all this way to let Pete Weston slip through my fingers while I sat there with some woman he raped. Hell, I've seen women after they been raped before. She'll be all right. Not like other's I've seen that were raped and then gutted like a pig!"

"You've changed, Alvin. You ain't the same man I rode with down on the Rio Grande."

"That was twelve years ago," Alvin scoffed. "Hell, I wasn't much more than a kid back then."

"I ain't talking about changes brought about by years. I'm talking about how you've changed on the inside. You had feelings back in those days. You cared about other folks."

"Yeah well, what do you expect after sixteen years of dealing with human garbage? When you're after men as no good and ruthless as Pete Weston, you best figure out how to be just as ruthless if you want to stay alive."

"I've seen plenty of ruthless men in my lifetime, Alvin. After Sherman burned his way across Georgia, I saw men that became so blinded by hatred that they couldn't think of anything except getting revenge. Some of them turned into animals...viscous animals...like wolves that kill for the sheer enjoyment of it. And I see you heading down that same road."

Both Alvin and Duv were silent for quite a while after that. Once the horses were no longer breathing hard, Alvin remounted and started his horse at constant lope and Duv followed. It was after sundown and the light was fading quickly by the time Pete's tracks reached the road between Alamogordo and Cloudcroft. Alvin and Duv guessed he would follow the road east to Cloudcroft, but the tracks crossed the road and continued in a northeasterly direction across open country.

"Might as well set up camp. Be dark soon," Alvin said as he slowed his horse. "We'll pick up his tracks again in the morning."

Alvin and Duv said little as they unsaddled their horses and went about setting up camp for the night. After gathering firewood, Alvin started a fire and put a pot of beans on the fire while Duv made coffee.

"You were right, Duv. I'm sorry. We should have stayed with

that woman until her husband got there," Alvin said later in an apologetic voice as he sat by the fire drinking coffee. "And you was right about some of the other things you said, too. When I first started rangerin', I wasn't hard like I am now. After a job was done, I could put it out of my mind, be happy, and friendly, and just be myself again. But here lately, seems like I just stay mad all the time. Kinda like today when I saw that woman after she'd been raped. All I felt was anger. Wasn't my fault she got raped. So, I didn't really feel anything for her. All I could do was think about catching up with the bastard that raped her and killing him!"

"Well, now that you ain't a Ranger no more...maybe you'll get back some of those feelings," Duv said calmly.

"I hope so, Duv. I really do."

Although both men were tired, neither of them slept well and they were both out of their bedrolls before the first rays of sunlight hit their camp. They saddled their horses, secured their bedrolls, and gear while the coffee cooked and once the coffee pot was empty, they continued following Pete's tracks. After about an hour, they came across a campfire that was still smoldering and the grass where Pete had rolled out his bedroll was still matted.

"You notice anything unusual?" Alvin asked after dismounting and looking around the campsite.

"Not really?" Duv replied as he looked around.

"There's no coffee grinds, or bread crumbs, or dried beans, or anything else in the way of scraps," Alvin said grinning. "He built a fire but he's got nothin' to eat."

"You're right, Alvin. I wouldn't have even noticed," Duv replied smiling. "I can tell you been at this awhile."

"Too long I'm afraid," Alvin replied.

"I reckon he was in such a hurry to leave after raping his brother's wife that he never even took time to gather up any grub for the trail," Duv said.

"Yeah, and the fact that he didn't go to Cloudcroft when he was this close... tells me he knows we're after him," Alvin said as he remounted his horse.

"He must have seen us when we were at the house the first time and hid out somewhere until we were gone."

"Yep, but he can't run for long without any supplies."

"He keeps pushing his horse the way he has been and he'll end up on foot, too," Duv added.

Alvin and Duv continued to follow Pete's tracks in a northeasterly direction for another half hour until they spotted dust rising in the distance. They stopped their horses and Alvin quickly pulled out his binoculars as several riders came over a distant ridge.

"They're soldiers!" Alvin said in a surprised voice after focusing his binoculars on the riders.

"Must be out on patrol," Duv said. "Maybe, they've seen Weston."

"Only one way to find out," Alvin said as he returned the binoculars to his saddlebags and spurred his horse.

When the cavalry men saw Alvin and Duv riding toward them, the lieutenant leading the column held up his hand and halted his men.

"What are you men doing out here?" the lieutenant asked as Alvin and Duv reached his position. "Don't you know this is the Mescalero Apache Reservation?"

"We're tracking a man that held up three stagecoaches and killed two men!" Alvin replied.

"Well, I'm afraid you'll have to turn back. No white men are allowed on the reservation without written permission from the commanding officer of Fort Stanton."

"Didn't you hear what I said, Lieutenant?" Alvin replied with an annoyed look. "We're after a man that killed two men, robbed two stagecoaches, and raped a woman!"

"I heard you, but my orders are to keep the Apaches on the reservation and keep all white men off," the lieutenant replied. "Where did all this robbing and killing take place, anyway?"

"In Texas," Alvin replied.

"You fellas bounty hunters?"

"I'm a former Texas Ranger," Alvin replied. "One of the men he killed was a friend of ours."

"The woman he raped just happened yesterday near Alamogordo... if that makes a difference," Duv added.

"What's his name?" the lieutenant asked. "I'll put it in my report."

"His name is Pete Weston, but the hell with your report! I want to catch the son of a bitch!" Alvin replied in an irritated voice.

"Sorry fellas, but I got my orders," the lieutenant said. "We'll keep an eye out for him while we're out here on patrol. If we don't find him...chances are the Apaches will. And if they do... you probably won't have to worry about seeing that he gets what's coming to him?"

"What if we go after him anyway?" Alvin asked in an angry tone.

"Well, I'm afraid I can't allow that. I'd have to place you under arrest and take you to Fort Stanton to face charges," the lieutenant replied. "Now you men have been warned. So, you best turn around and ride back the same way you came."

"I guess there's nothing else we can do, Duv," Alvin said in a dejected voice as he turned his horse and started it back toward the way they had come.

"You ain't really headin' back are you, Alvin?" Duv asked once they were out of ear shot and the cavalry patrol continued on its way.

"Hell no! I figure once we pick up Weston's trail again and those blue coats get over that rise yonder, we'll turn around and keep after him," Alvin replied. "Best be on the lookout for Apaches, though."

"Yeah, sounds like they don't take kindly to trespassers."

Once Alvin and Duv were back to the spot where they had left Pete's trail, they resumed following his tracks deeper into the Apache's reservation. In order to keep from kicking up any dust, rather than galloping after Pete, they kept their horses at a steady trot.

"You see those buzzards up ahead, Alvin?"

"Yeah, I just noticed them. Maybe, we best dismount before we get much closer and sneak up there on foot and take a look."

Alvin and Duv dismounted and after tying their horses to a couple of sage bushes, they pulled their Winchesters. They crouched low and weaved their way through the sage until they were close to the top of a low ridge that prevented them from seeing what the buzzards were circling. Then they dropped down to their knees and crawled the last few feet until they could see the other side. Below the ridge, in a dry wash, they could see a horse lying in the sand, still saddled, near death, but occasionally raising its head, refusing to give up.

"Son of bitch rode it into the ground and didn't even have enough decency to put a bullet in its brain," Duv said with a disgusted expression.

"Probably didn't want to risk anybody hearing the shot," Alvin replied.

"Well, it shouldn't take long for us to catch up to him now. Looks like his track are heading straight down that draw."

Alvin and Duv were just about to stand up and return to their horses when Duv caught a glimpse of movement out of the corner of his eye. He grabbed Alvin's arm and pulled him down just as an Apache brave, riding a brown and white paint, with a trapdoor carbine across his lap, appeared on the ridge across the wash.

"Looks like we ain't the only ones that spotted those buzzards," Duv whispered to Alvin.

The Apache stopped his horse on the ridge and put his hand to his forehead to shield his eyes from the intense sun as he gazed at the dying horse. After spending a few minutes on the ridge looking around, hoping to spot the man who had abandoned the horse, but seeing nothing, the Apache nudged his horse forward and cautiously rode down into the draw. He stopped his horse near the dying horse and quickly jumped down from the paint. The dying horse raised its head and looked at the Apache as he spoke softly and stroked the horse's head. Then the Apache quickly pulled his knife, buried it in the horse's neck, and slit its throat to end the horse's suffering. As the sand at his feet turned red, the Apache's eyes followed the footprints down the wash. Then he returned the knife to its sheath and walked to his paint. After swinging up onto the paint's back, he started it forward with the heels of his moccasins, and followed the footprints down the wash. Alvin and Duv remained where they were until the Apache disappeared around a bend at the far end of the wash.

"Let's get back to our horses," Alvin whispered.

"I'll be right behind you," Duv replied.

Alvin and Duv returned to their horses and after stuffing their Winchesters back in the saddle scabbards, they walked back to the draw with their horses in tow. When they reached the dead horse, they mounted their horses and cautiously began following Pete's footprints and the tracks left by the Apache.

They were just about to the bend in the wash when they heard a shot followed quickly by a second coming from over the ridge on their right.

"Those didn't sound like they came from a trapdoor carbine," Alvin said.

"They sure didn't!" Duv replied.

Alvin and Duv spurred their horses and rode toward the top of ridge, stopping just short of the crest to dismount. They ran the last few feet on foot and drop down on their bellies as they reached the crest of the ridge. Less than a quarter mile away, they spotted Pete on the brown and white paint horse feverishly galloping toward the north. Then suddenly a band of Apaches appeared out of a draw a short distance in front of him. Pete reined the paint around and started it galloping back toward the wash. The Apaches let out a series of yelps and immediately gave chase. Pete fired the last four rounds from his pistol in hopes of ending their pursuit, but the hastily fired rounds did nothing to discourage the whooping and hollering Apaches. By all accounts, Pete was an excellent rider, but he was no match for the six Apaches who had spent their entire lives riding bareback and were now chasing him across rough and open terrain. By the time Pete was within a hundred yards of the wash, the Apaches were only a few yards behind him. Alvin and Duv knew that the Apaches could have easily ended the chase with a single bullet, but it was obvious that they wanted Pete alive. When the brown and white paint plunged down the ridge into the wash, it stumbled in the loose sand and Pete was thrown. Before he could get to his feet, the six Apaches were already on him, punching, and kicking him until he quit resisting. Then they tore off all of his clothes and dragged him to a dead pinion at the side of the wash. Once his arms and feet were tightly bound to the twisted trunk with rawhide, one of the Apaches grabbed Pete by the hair and drew his knife as if he were going to scalp him alive, but before he could drag his knife across Pete's forehead; one of the other Indians grabbed his arm. The two braves argued in their native tongue while the other four watched. After arguing for a few minutes, the two braves settled their differences and started laughing. The other four braves joined in the laughter as more words were spoken. Then the one who had drawn his knife walked back to Pete and kicked him in groin. Pete screamed out in agony, straining to bend over, but the rawhide held him upright. The Apaches laughed again, but their laughter was quickly drowned out by Pete's screams as the Apache started making a series of cuts across Pete's chest from his arm pits to his sternum. His screams continued as the Apache began peeling back the skin with the tip of his knife.

"My god they're gonna skin him alive," Duv whispered, his face grimacing.

"What are you doing?" Alvin whispered as Duv started to slithered back down the bank.

"I'm gonna put a bullet in his brain," Duv said as he stood up and walked to his horse.

"You shoot him now and you'll have that whole bunch of savages chasing us to get satisfaction."

"Maybe so, but I'm not like you, Alvin. I can't just watch a man get skinned alive and tortured to death," Duv said as he pulled the Winchester from his saddle scabbard.

"Put the rifle down!" Alvin said as he pulled his pistol and aimed it at Duv.

Duv stared at Alvin in disbelief, wondering if Alvin had finally gone mad.

"You'd shoot me, Alvin?" Duv asked refusing to believe his eyes.

"Weston deserves to die!" Alvin said in an angry voice.

"I got no problem killing him, Alvin...But no man deserves to die like that," Duv said as Pete let out another blood curdling scream.

"I mean it Duv, put the rifle down!" Alvin said cocking his

pistol.

Duv stared at Alvin slowly shaking his head for a moment still refusing to believe that Alvin would actually shoot him. Then he shoved the rifle back into the scabbard and after giving Alvin one last glaring look, Duv put his foot in the stirrup and swung up into the saddle, reined his horse around, and started it back down the ridge at a fast trot. He had only gone a short distance up the wash when the crack of a rifle echoed between the ridges paralleling the wash. Duv pulled his horse to a stop and turned around in the saddle. A moment later, Alvin's horse appeared in the wash racing at a full gallop with Alvin leaning forward in the saddle, feverishly whipping the ends of the reins across his horse's rump.

"Better put the spurs to that nag if you want to keep your hair!" Alvin shouted as he rode by.

Duv quickly glanced over his shoulder again as he heard Apache war cries behind him. When he saw the six Apaches coming around the bend in the wash, he started his horse galloping after Alvin yelling, "There may be hope for you yet, Alvin Witherspoon!"

After a long chase, Alvin and Duv managed to outrun the Apaches, but they continued pushing their horses until they were well beyond the boundaries of the reservation.

"Damn you, Duv! That was too close," Alvin said as he pulled his horse to a stop and dismounted.

"What are you cussing me for?" Duv asked laughing as he also dismounted. "You were the one that pulled the trigger."

"Yeah, but it was your idea!"

"Admit it, Alvin...you know it was the right thing to do."

"Yeah, I know it. I guess I just wasn't thinking clear," Alvin replied as he started walking his horse to cool it off. "I'm sorry I pulled a gun on you, Duv. I hope you'll forgive me."

"I forgive you. I doubt you would have shot me, anyhow."

"Well, it's good to have it over with!" Alvin said with a relieved look. "I can't wait to get back to the ranch."

"Yeah me too, but I figure we got one more thing to do before we start back to Texas." Duv said looking at Alvin.

"What's that?" Alvin asked with as puzzled look.

"I figure we owe it to Pete's brother to let him know Pete's dead. And it still bothers me that we rode off and just left his brother's wife like we did. I'd like to make sure she's okay and apologize to her for not staying with her until her husband got there."

Alvin glanced at Duv with a guilty expression on his face but did not reply. Then he looked away and stared at the dirt as he continued leading his horse.

"I mean it, Alvin!" Duv said after Alvin remained silent. "If you don't want to go...I'll just go without you."

"Like hell you will!" Alvin replied with a remorseful look and a weak smile. "I'm going, too. It's about time I start acting like a human being again."

After a brief stop at Grant's ranch, Alvin and Duv continued on their journey back to Texas. They arrived at the Double M Ranch a few days later to a warm reception. Whether or not Pete Weston had actually been killed never came up in conversation. But, everyone knew that Duv and Alvin's return meant that Punch's murder had been avenged in one way or another. Some, like Luke, took comfort in knowing that Punch's murderer had been killed while others, like Willow, were merely thankful for the closure that it brought her. Regardless of their personal feelings, everyone was happy that Duv and Alvin had returned safely and they were eager to see things return to normal on the Double M. Alvin took Willow up on her offer to make the Double M Ranch his home and over time he and Lucy became more than just friends. They were married exactly two years after Alvin resigned from the Rangers and Willow's first grandson, Austin Punch Masters, was born on Christmas day of the following year.

The End

A note from the author, Norm Bass:
Thanks for reading *Beyond the Pecos* and helping to keep the spirit of the old west alive. I hope you enjoyed the book. You can e-mail me directly at hookedb@hotmail.com or follow me on Twitter.

Other Books by Norm Bass:
Justice Rides A Spotted Horse
Beneath The Rustler's Moon (Vol. I - The Gentry Brothers Series)
Tin Cup Justice (Vol. II - The Gentry Brothers Series)
They Hung An Innocent Man (Vol. III - The Gentry Brothers Series)
Cactus Casanovas
South Of The Pecos

Made in the USA
Charleston, SC
13 January 2013